THE KINGFISHER BOOK OF

TALES FROM RUSSIA

James Mayhew

NEW YORK

For Mari and Gabriel Benedict Giacomo, with love

Author's Acknowledgments

Thanks to Gina Pollinger and Caroline Walsh for all their support, my mother for her ideas, my wife Mari for finding references, and to all at Kingfisher for their help in producing this revised edition. The following were my main sources for the stories:

Operatic libretti

Bel'sky, V.I. after A. Pushkin *The Tale of Tsar Saltan, of his son the famous and heroic Prince Guidon Saltanovitch and of the Beautiful Swan Princess* (1901)
Bel'sky, V.I./N.A. Rimsky-Korsakov *Sadko* (1897)
Petrovsky, E.M./N.A. Rimsky-Korsakov *Kastchey the Immortal* (1902)
Rimsky-Korsakov, N.A. after A.N. Ostrovsky *Snegoorotchka* (1881)

Books

Bain, R. Nisbet *Russian Fairy Tales,* selected from the *skazki* of Polevoi (Lawrence & Bullen, 1892)
Steele, Robert, ed. *The Russian Garland,* from chapbooks made in Moscow. Ill. J.R. De Rosciszewski (Bride, Nast & Co. Ltd., 1916)
Wheeler, Post *Russian Wonder Tales* Ill. Bilibin (A & C Black Ltd., 1912)

KINGFISHER
Larousse Kingfisher Chambers Inc.
95 Madison Avenue
New York, New York 10016

First published in 1993
First published in paperback in 2000
2 4 6 8 10 9 7 5 3 1
1TR/0600/WKT/(MA)/KTMA115

LIBRARY OF CONGRESS CATALOGING-IN-PUBLICATION DATA
has been applied for.

ISBN 0-7534-5293-6

Printed in Hong Kong

Contents

I

Tsar Saltan and Koshka the Cat 4

We meet Tsar Saltan and Koshka the cat, who tells the tale of

THE SNOWMAIDEN 10

II

Tsar Saltan and Koshka the Cat 19

Koshka the storytelling cat tells the tale of

SADKO THE MINSTREL 23

III

Tsar Saltan and Koshka the Cat 33

Koshka tells the tale of

THE FIREBIRD, IVAN, AND GRAY WOLF 37

IV

Tsar Saltan and Koshka the Cat 52

Koshka tells the most powerful tale of all

VASSILISA THE FAIR AND BABA-YAGA 57

V

Tsar Saltan and Koshka the Cat 70

Koshka's own tale is at last told

Author's Note 80

I
Tsar Saltan and Koshka the Cat

THERE WAS A TIME, long ago, when the land of Russia was divided up into many parts. Each had a ruler called a tsar, so each was called a tsardom. The great and distinguished Tsar Saltan Saltanovich had a fine tsardom, and he ruled it well, but he had no tsaritsa to rule beside him. So he traveled far and wide in search of a woman worthy of the throne.

Finally he came upon the very last house in his tsardom. He stood outside in the snow, stroked his beard, and listened. There were three orphaned sisters inside, and by chance they were each imagining that Tsar Saltan had chosen her for his bride.

"If the tsar chose me," said Katooshka, the eldest sister, "I would weave silk clothes, finer than any in the world."

"Is that so?" said the second sister, Liza Poffarikha. "If the tsar chose me I would bake better bread than any he has yet tasted."

Then the two sisters said to the youngest, "What would you give to Tsar Saltan if he were to marry you?"

"Well," began the youngest sister, whose name was Militrissa, "as I cannot weave silk or bake bread, I would bear him seven heroic golden-haired sons to sit beside his throne."

Tsar Saltan thought for a while. "My own clothes are very good as it is, and the bread at the palace isn't so bad." So he opened the

door of the little house and chose Militrissa as his wife, for he longed for heroic sons such as those she had promised.

The wedding feast lasted for three days and three nights, and on the fourth day Tsar Saltan and Tsaritsa Militrissa went to live in the tsar's palace. But the two elder sisters were poisoned with envy. Even when the tsar asked them to live in the palace as royal seamstress and cook, their hatred for their little sister filled every vein in their bodies and every thought in their heads. When Tsaritsa Militrissa announced that she was to be a mother, the two sisters were beside themselves with rage. Katooshka threw her sister's dough to the ground, and Liza Poffarikha tore at her sister's silks.

"They say an old witch called Baba-Yaga Bony-Legs, who knows all things, lives deep in the forest," said Katooshka at last. "Maybe she will help us." The two of them blew their red noses and set off.

The witch could smell them coming through the thorny trees.

"No more water, no more mud,
Tonight I'll drink some human blood!"

she croaked. And when the two sisters found her, they dared not even knock upon her door, for her hut jumped around on chicken's legs and was surrounded by a fence of human bones.

"Come in, children, so I can eat you," crooned Baba-Yaga.

"Wait, Grandma," said Katooshka. "Dear sweet Babooshka, we need the help that only your wisdom can provide."

Baba-Yaga let the two sisters in and was so flattered that she did not attempt to eat them. They told her the tale of Militrissa, the tsar and the seven golden-haired sons and begged for help.

"You must pretend to love your sister dearly, and the tsar will put his trust in you," said the witch. "Tell him to go to battle, and when each child is born, bring him to me. Put what you like in the

cradle, and when the tsar returns he will see that the tsaritsa produces monsters for children. By the time the seventh prince is born the tsar will tire of her and throw her into the sea."

The sisters returned to the palace and began their scheming.

"I hear there is to be a battle in the South," said Katooshka.

"Indeed it is so," said Liza Poffarikha. "And it is the tsar's duty to lead his army." Weeping and wailing they embraced Militrissa.

Trusting that his wife would be well looked after by such loving sisters, the tsar put on his armor, gathered his army, and set off upon his horse.

Militrissa wept night and day without pause, while the two evil sisters hid their laughter and pretended to share Militrissa's sadness.

Soon enough Tsaritsa Militrissa gave birth to triplets, each baby a heroic golden-haired son, just as she had promised her husband. While she slept, her sisters took the babies from the cradle and gave them to Baba-Yaga. In their place they left three puppies.

A message was sent to the tsar, and he returned to find his two wicked sisters-in-law waiting outside his wife's bedchamber.

"Sire, do not enter here!" wept Katooshka.

"Do not harm our sister," wailed Liza Poffarikha.

"What can you mean?" demanded the tsar. "Why should I harm my own dear wife?"

"Because she has given birth to puppies!" said Katooshka.

"And you will probably want to cast her into the sea in a barrel!" said Liza Poffarikha.

Militrissa was horrified to find her beloved sons had turned into puppies, and the tsar did indeed have them cast into the sea. But Militrissa he loved, and so forgave. Militrissa was greatly relieved to have such a forgiving husband and never mentioned the puppies.

Time passed, and soon all was happy as before. But one day

Militrissa announced that she was to be a mother once more. Right away Katooshka wept and said, "There is to be a battle in the West."

"It will be the tsar's duty to go," wailed Liza Poffarikha.

So the tsar put on his armor, gathered his army, and rode off to battle, believing his wife to be in the safe hands of her loving sisters.

At length, Militrissa gave birth to twin sons, each heroic and golden-haired as she had promised her husband. But while she slept the princes were taken to Baba-Yaga and this time replaced with kittens.

A message was sent to the tsar, and when he returned he found his two sisters-in-law wailing and weeping. They told him that his fair wife had borne kittens, and the tsar ordered them to be cast into the sea. But Militrissa he forgave, for he loved her deeply. She thought herself very fortunate to have such an understanding husband, and so never once did she mention the kittens.

Time passed, and all was happy again as before. But no sooner had the Tsaritsa Militrissa announced that she would soon be a mother again than the two elder sisters burst into tears.

"There is to be a battle in the North," said one.

"The tsar must go, it is his duty," said the other.

Once more the tsar put on his armor and led his army into battle, leaving the tsaritsa with her sisters.

After a while, Militrissa gave birth to two more princely sons. But she was clever this time and said only one child had been born, and sent this message to the tsar. The second child she hid up her sleeve, and she told not a soul about him. While she slept her sisters took the first prince, and in his place they threw a loaf of bread baked by the one, wrapped in cloth woven by the other.

When the tsar returned, his sisters-in-law were waiting for him.

"Sire, it is horrible," said Katooshka, blowing her nose.

"No puppy or kitten this," said Liza Poffarikha. "Our tsaritsa has produced a monster words cannot describe."

This time the tsar flew into a rage. Even his love for Militrissa could not endure such a test, and he ordered that the tsaritsa be cast into the sea along with the bread! The sisters were almost inside out with mirth. They jumped and they hopped and they danced all the way to Baba-Yaga's hut with the sixth tsarevich. But in front of the tsaritsa they pretended to be desolate that such a fate awaited her.

That night Militrissa was put into a casket, with the bread, by the tsar's own guards, and this was hurled from the highest cliff into the cold ocean far below, for all eternity.

But the casket did not sink, and Militrissa did not perish. She took her golden-haired baby son from her sleeve, and for many days the two of them floated upon the open sea where neither sun nor moon found its way inside the casket. On and on it floated, tossed by storms and sea monsters. It seemed to Militrissa that the prince, whom she had called Guidon, grew not by the day but by the hour, for already he was a heroic lad. She clothed him in the one sister's cloth and fed him the other's bread, and passed the time by telling him how they came to be imprisoned in a casket.

At length it became cramped in the casket, so as soon as Militrissa was certain that there was dry land beneath them, Guidon pushed with all his strength and broke the casket apart. Looking around them, they blinked in the sunshine, which Militrissa had forgotten and Guidon had never seen. They saw that they were upon a small island, where the only thing that grew was a mighty oak tree upon a hill. As they sat beneath its wide branches to rest, they saw a golden chain all around the tree and on the end of it an old black cat.

"Greetings, lovely Tsaritsa and noble Prince," said the cat, who

guessed from Militrissa's clothes that they were royalty. "I have waited many years for guests, but I did not expect such distinguished visitors." She climbed down and bowed her head solemnly. "Can I be of service to you?" she asked.

"Well maybe you can, Koshka," said the tsarevich, who could see this was no ordinary black cat. "Can you tell us the way to Tsar Saltan's palace?"

"If you catch me a fish I can tell you what I know," said the cat. Young Guidon took wood from the casket and fashioned a spear. He caught a fish and gave it to old black Koshka. She was a kind-hearted cat, and when the fish was baked she shared it with the tsaritsa and her son.

Then she washed carefully behind her ears and said, "This is the Island of Bouyan, and Tsar Saltan's realm is far over the seven blue seas and beyond the thrice-ninth tsardom. One day a ship will pass by here, but whether it will help you or not is hard to say."

"What, then, should we do?" asked Guidon.

"Perhaps you should listen to me tell you a tale," said Koshka, turning left. "Or sing you a song," she added, turning right.

"Can you truly tell us a tale?" said the prince, who was not used to such wonders as a storytelling cat.

"I can tell many tales," said the cat. "And sing many songs."

"The song of a cat is hard to appreciate," said Militrissa. "But a tale would be welcome to help pass the time."

"I will tell the tale of the Snowmaiden," said Koshka, and she walked again to the left, washed her whiskers, and began her tale.

The Snowmaiden

Far away, in the North, lies the land of the Midnight Sun. All through the summer, every hour of the day is filled with golden sunshine. But when Old Father Frost passes by, the sun goes to sleep and the earth lies cold and dead for the whole winter long.

A woodcutter, named Boris, and his wife, Bobilika, had lived there for many years in a little wooden house, just the two of them. But the house was always quiet because they had no children, and their lives seemed empty without a little one of their own. This was their only sadness, but it was as big and as wide as old Mother Russia herself.

Winter came, and the sun slept. Boris was busy cutting trees for the village folk to burn in their stoves. Bobilika stayed inside making hot soup for her husband's return each evening.

One bleak day it was much colder than usual. Bobilika sat by the kitchen window to watch the children from the village playing in the snow and to dream her dreams of spring. The snow fell steadily, and each flake seemed more beautiful than the one before. Bobilika said to herself:

"If I had a daughter, she would be as fair as a snowflake."

When Boris came home that evening, he called to his wife: "Bobilika! The children have built a snowman. Come and see."

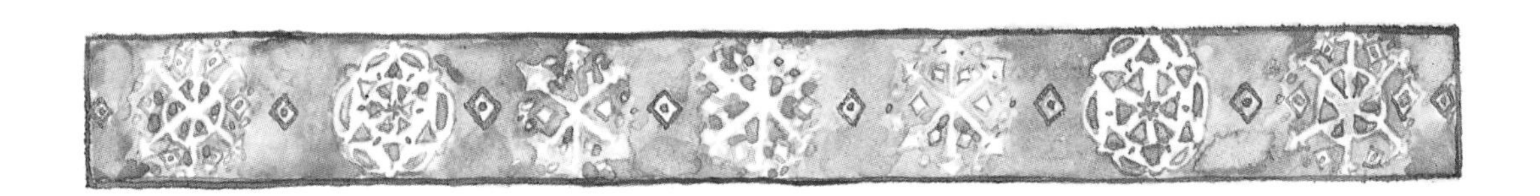

Bobilika put on her furriest hat and her warmest coat. It really was very cold outside that evening, and it hurt to breathe. The whole forest looked as if it were made of sugar frosting.

The snowman had coals for his eyes and a beet for his nose.

"We could make a better one," said Boris, teasing. He started to build a snow figure, knowing that his wife would interfere.

Bobilika shook her head. "It's all wrong. You start with a small ball of snow, and you roll it along to make it bigger." They rolled their snowball into the forest, and the Northern Lights flickered in the shining green sky.

"A large ball of snow for the body," said Bobilika.

"And a little one for the head," said Boris.

The sky had grown deep blue with cold, but neither Bobilika nor Boris cared. A little more carving here, some whittling and smoothing there...and...what was this? It was no snowman they had built, but a snowmaiden. A beautiful little child, white and frozen. Without knowing it, Bobilika and Boris had carved their hearts' desire, a daughter, out of the snow. But the cold pinched at their toes and fingers, so they followed their footsteps back to the cottage and warmed some cabbage soup on the stove.

The sky turned black and was alive with stars. Father Frost was passing through the forest, and the air seemed brittle with cold, crackling around his ears. As he shuffled past, with his long frozen beard and purple nose, he saw the little Snowmaiden, sparkling between the trees.

Yet she could not move or speak, and Frost, the bringer of Winter, could not give life, only take it away. But his eyes gleamed, and he smiled a wide smile. "Mother Spring!" he called, "Where is my spring beauty?" His voice sounded like the wind, and it shook the icicles from the trees and the snow from the rooftops,

and right away Mother Spring was there beside Frost.

"Can't you manage without me then?" she said, shivering.

"I can freeze things perfectly," said Frost coldly. "But only you can give life."

Spring laughed. "It's a bit early in the year," she said, "but what is it to be? A flower, some trees?"

"The Snowmaiden," said Frost. "She can be our little child, the daughter of Winter and Spring!"

"And what of those who made her?" asked Spring.

"They may have her for now," said Frost. "But she will come to us one day soon — you just wait and see."

So Spring took a deep breath and blew a warm breeze onto the frozen figure. Then before they could be seen, Frost and Spring drifted off through the forest.

Bobilika drank her hot soup and looked out of the window at the little Snowmaiden. She could just see her, shining white in the dark forest.

"If I had a daughter," she said to herself, "she would be as fair as a snowflake." And the strangest thing happened. The little child, made out of snow, smiled back at her.

Bobilika shouted to her husband, "She is alive!" And she ran out of the door and danced upon the snow like a flame in the stove.

"But she's only snow and ice," said Boris, running after her. He brushed some snow off the little

child. There was a lock of hair and her shining eyes, blue like a spring sky. Quickly he brushed off more snow — there were her hands and feet, in mittens and boots. She really was alive, just like you or me.

Of course she was only made out of snow, and her little heart was frozen. But she was alive just the same.

At last Boris found his tongue and said, "Who are you? Where are you from?"

"I'm Snegoorotchka," she answered.

"Sne...Goo..." spluttered Boris.

"Rotchka!" laughed the child. "Sne...goo...rotchka!"

"She's called Snegoorotchka, the little Snowmaiden," said Bobilika, "because we made her out of snow." She wrapped her shawl around the child, and they took her home, pinching themselves all over in case it turned out to be a dream.

But no dream of theirs was as wonderful as the Snowmaiden. Even they could not have imagined anyone so beautiful. Everyone fell under her spell, the children most of all. She enchanted them with stories about the cold North, and she glittered and dazzled like the glassy forests they sped past on their sleighs. Snegoorotchka could command the snowflakes to take on any form: delicate frosted flowers, whole gardens of ice ferns, and strange winter animals. All of them silent and magnificent.

And how Snegoorotchka danced when the shepherd played his flute for her. She could whirl around like a snowflake, making everyone dizzy!

Yet, as time passed, the children all noticed that the Snowmaiden was a little strange. She was beautiful and clever, that was true, but she wouldn't sit by the fire or drink hot soup. She was a melancholic child, cold and distant. And however much the children loved her, she remained unloving and unfeeling. She liked to listen to the shepherd boy play his flute, but all the others — she could take them or leave them.

The weeks passed by. Whether it was a long time or not, it's hard to say, for a tale is quick to tell yet time passes slowly. Winter came to an end, and everyone put away their fur hats. Before long the snow began to melt from the meadows, and as the patches of white became smaller, the green grass grew longer. Soon it was bright, warm springtime.

Snegoorotchka stayed inside, afraid to go out any more, and not even the shepherd could persuade her. Instead he sang songs about the little Snowmaiden, whose face was as pale as the moon. "She is so lonely," he thought. "If only she'd let me love her."

Bobilika grew worried. "Why so sad?" she asked, placing a twist of flowers in the Snowmaiden's hair. "You should be glad to see spring awaken the flowers and to hear the birdsong."

But Snegoorotchka seemed sadder with each new day. How the falling apple blossom and the snowdrops reminded her of her beloved snow. Yet they were spirits of springtime. She wept for the melting snow, and they were not tears that fell from her eyes, but snowflakes.

Even though spring had come, the Sun had not yet appeared in the sky. One by one the flowers opened their petals to greet the Sun, only to find the sky was cold and gray.

The truth was that the Sun was angry. Angry because it was time for summer, and yet there remained in the forest a spirit of winter, whose heart was frozen.

Soon it was midsummer. On this, the longest of days, a big festival took place in the forest.

"You must come to the dance, little Snegoorotchka!" said Boris. "It will be fun."

"There will be bonfires and games," said Bobilika.

"Music and songs," shouted Boris.

"Tales to be told," whispered Bobilika.

"And the Hopak to be danced!" Boris took up his balalaika and played for Bobilika.

But the Snowmaiden knew nothing about summer festivals, so she hid in the dark forest away from the music and laughter.

The shepherd boy soon noticed that the little Snowmaiden was not there. He missed her pale face, her slender arms, her sad blue eyes. He played his flute, over and over, and peered through the windows of Boris's little house.

At last he went looking for Snegoorotchka in the forest.

The Snowmaiden sat by a cool brook that twisted around the trees, and she did not hear the shepherd steal up behind her. Gently he took her hand and then danced with her as he played his flute. How graceful she was, how pale and beautiful. But the Snowmaiden was afraid of him, and her heart was just as frozen now as in midwinter.

Round and round the shepherd spun her, and at the end of the dance he leaned forward and kissed her on the lips. Snegoorotchka looked into the shepherd's warm, kind eyes, and in that instant she fell in love and her heart was melted. "Come to the dance," said the shepherd. "Come dance the Hopak with me!"

Such was the noise of festival, with all the singing and dancing and laughter, that the Sun could not resist taking a glance over the horizon. His eyes fell upon the little Snowmaiden.

Snegoorotchka was no longer afraid of the warm summer air. She twirled and sparkled in the bright sunshine as she danced to the music. Poor Snowmaiden! The Sun would not shine while her heart was frozen, but love had melted her heart, and now the sunlight went right through her.

She let out a little sigh and tears fell from her eyes — not snowflakes, but real warm tears! She slipped from the shepherd boy's warm arms, kissed his hand, and was gone. The Snowmaiden had melted into a summer mist.

The shepherd played his flute to try to bring her back, but she did not return. The villagers looked in the dark forests, and by the cool streams, but there was no sign of her.

Boris and Bobilika said nothing. They realized that their little Snegoorotchka really had been made out of snowflakes. She was a spirit of winter and had no place in the summertime.

But the Snowmaiden wasn't dead, for spirits can never die. She had gone to the North Pole, to live with Old Father Frost in his frozen white palace.

So the Sun returned and everyone was warm. Boris and Bobilika walked slowly home. "Once we had a daughter, and she was as fair as a snowflake," said Bobilika to Boris. "Yet it is hard to feel sad or lonely when the Sun is shining."

And perhaps next winter, when Old Father Frost comes to the forest with his cold blanket of snow, who knows? Maybe then, Snegoorotchka, the little Snowmaiden, will come back to them.

II

Tsar Saltan and Koshka the Cat

KOSHKA THE CAT washed her paws and blinked slowly. Militrissa lay back on the soft grass and felt the warm spring sun on her face. "It was a sad tale," she said. "More sad than happy."

"But there can be no real happiness without sadness," said Koshka. "For if we are never sad, how can we recognize happiness?"

"You are a wise and clever cat," said Guidon, stroking Koshka.

"In that case, you may catch me a fish, for I know many happy tales, but a starving cat will remember only sad ones."

Guidon ran to the beach with his spear and soon caught a fish. The three of them had barely started to eat it when the young tsarevich saw something far out on the sparkling blue ocean. It was the ship they had been waiting for!

"Quickly, Mother, to the beach," shouted the prince.

The ship drew close to the island.

"Greetings," called Militrissa. "Tell me, where are you bound?"

An elderly merchant from the ship told her they were headed east, over the sea and beyond the thrice-nine tsardoms to the realm of Tsar Saltan the Magnificent.

"May we come with you?" asked the prince.

"Alas, the ship is laden with silks and other cloths for the tsar.

Another stitch and we would surely all sink and drown."

"It does not matter," said Militrissa. "Perhaps we would not be welcome there, though the tsar would be most welcome to visit the Island of Bouyan. Here there lives an enchanted cat, and when on the right of the tree, she sings. Better still, if she turns to the left she tells stories."

"Is that so?" said the old merchant.

"It is," said Militrissa. "Be sure to have a safe journey, friends, and to tell Tsar Saltan Saltanovich that which I have told you. Who knows, it may set him longing to visit the island."

The merchants sailed away across the seven seas, where terrible storms threw them about, and beyond the thrice-nine realms. After many days and nights they at last came to a safe port in the tsardom of Saltan Saltanovich.

The tsar was delighted with the silks and cloths and invited the merchants to his palace, where he provided a magnificent feast. There were musicians and storytellers, and all the royal household was invited. Among them sat Katooshka, still royal seamstress, and Liza Poffarikha, cook to the tsar.

"Good merchant," said the tsar to the oldest guest, "you have sailed the seven seas and oceans. Tell me, of all the marvels you have seen, what sight or discovery excited you most?"

"Mighty Tsar, we saw many wonders, but that which excited us most was that which we expected the least," said the old merchant. "Beyond the thrice-nine tsardoms there lies the Island of Bouyan. Upon a green hill, under a mighty oak tree, we saw a lady of uncommon beauty and her fine golden-haired son, who invite you to visit their humble place. There they live with old black Koshka. This cat sings when to the right of the tree and, when to the left, tells stories."

"It is a very kind invitation," said the Tsar. "I should indeed like to hear this cat tell me a tale."

The two sisters were at once suspicious, for they knew Militrissa had only had six of the promised seven golden-haired sons. What if she had survived to have a seventh?

They quickly made their way to the hut of old Baba-Yaga, for they dared not let the tsar visit the isle.

"Sweet Grandma, you must help us," they wailed, and they told Baba-Yaga the whole story.

"You must help yourselves," said Baba-Yaga. "Ask the tsar to command the merchant to return to the island and beg the cat to tell the tale of a minstrel named Sadko. The cat cannot know this tale. It is a tale of wonder that only I know. When this cat cannot tell the tale, the tsar will no longer wish to go to the island. Now be off or I shall gobble up the pair of you."

The two sisters returned to the palace and found the tsar all packed and ready to go. Katooshka stood on her toes and whispered into the tsar's ear, "Sire, do not go on a fool's errand. This story of a tale-telling cat is but lies and deceit."

So the tsar said to the old merchant, "How can I know the tale you have told is true?"

"I can only tell you that which has been told to my own ears," said the merchant.

Then Liza Poffarikha stood on her toes and whispered in the tsar's other ear. "Sire, command the merchant to return to the isle and beg the cat to tell the tale of the minstrel named Sadko, for this is a tale of wonder that no one knows. If the cat can tell the story, it is a marvel indeed."

The tsar called his storytellers to him and asked each in turn if they knew the tale of Sadko. But none had ever heard of such a

story, so the tsar agreed to the plan and commanded the old merchant accordingly. As soon as the feasting was over the merchants set sail to the west.

Time passed, and the merchant's ship, returning from its voyage across the seven seas and oceans, at last came upon the Island of Bouyan once more. Militrissa welcomed them, and together they feasted on baked fish.

"How was the mighty Tsar Saltan?" asked the tsaritsa.

"My lady, the tsar was well," said the old merchant. "We told him of our travels and he was charmed by your invitation to hear a story from the tale-telling cat. However, before he accepts he needs some proof that such a tale is true."

"Let me aboard and I will tell the tsar myself!" said Guidon.

"Alas, the ship carries mead and wine for the tsar. A single drop more and we would all sink and drown," said the old merchant.

"We may not be welcome there in any case," said Militrissa, "so you must hear our friend the wise cat tell a tale." They climbed the hill and sat beneath the mighty oak tree.

"Kind Koshka, tell us a tale," said Prince Guidon.

"With pleasure," said the wise black cat, who liked a large audience. "What tale would you like to hear?"

"Wise and wonderful animal," said the old merchant, "tell us the tale of the minstrel named Sadko."

"I know this tale well," said Koshka. She stretched herself and walked around the mighty oak tree, to the left. Then she sat down, and with her tail neatly curled around her velvet paws, she began.

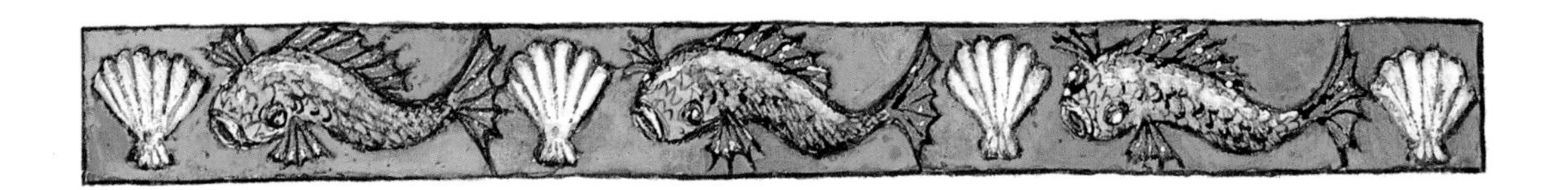

Sadko the Minstrel

In the fair city of Novgorod, far from the seven seas, a wealthy trader died and left not a single kopeck to his son. Instead he bequeathed him a goosli, a beautiful musical instrument made out of maple wood. It is like a little harp, except that you lay it down upon your lap to play it. But it was not a valuable instrument, and so his son, who was named Sadko, was quite poor.

Sadko was no fool, though, and he soon learned to play the goosli. He played it like no one before or since and made a small living from the kopecks that the rich merchants tossed into his cap when he played at their feasts. But one day no one asked Sadko to play at a feast or a banquet, and so he caught no money in his hat. No one cared that he went hungry. The same thing happened the next day and for a third day after that. So Sadko played his goosli just for himself — and who can blame him for that?

He would sit on the leafy green banks of Lake Ilmen, in the moonlight, and sing softly to himself. Sometimes, if he was lucky, he caught a fish, which made a very good supper, and so he lived.

Well, it just so happened that one clear night, when the moon was smiling in the sky, Sadko heard a voice singing back. It was a sweet, clear voice, and Sadko believed it to be a rusalka or water sprite, the ghost of a drowned maiden whose heart had been broken.

Sadko stopped his playing and looked down into the still water. A beautiful girl smiled back at him. Yet this was no rusalka, for she was dressed in silver, pearls, and seashells with golden pieces hanging down. It was the Princess Volkova, whose father was the Tsar of the Sea. She had been so charmed by Sadko's music that she had fallen in love with him.

"Play me another song," she said rising out of the water. Sadko played on, and the princess danced upon the surface of the lake. The minstrel had never seen anyone so lovely, and when he finished his song the princess came over to him and said shyly, "Thank you for that beautiful playing. Now I shall give you something in return." She took three gold pieces from her dress and threw them into the lake. "When you next cast your nets here," she said, "you will catch three fish, each with fins of gold, which will bring you great wealth." Then she disappeared beneath the waters.

Sadko wasted no time at all in returning to Novgorod to get his biggest fishing net. If there were fish with golden fins, he wanted to catch them before anyone else did.

But on his way he was stopped by Vladimir, a merchant. "Minstrel, will you play at my banquet tonight?" he asked.

"I have to catch fish with fins of gold," said Sadko.

"You would turn down good work for fairy tales?" said Vladimir. Well, Sadko could see that a cap full of money was the thing to have, so he agreed to play. The golden fish could wait.

At the banquet, all the wealthy merchants of Novgorod ate and drank, and then drank and ate. Vladimir stood up and said: "A toast to Sadko the minstrel, who thinks he can catch fish with golden fins!"

"*What?*" said a Viking merchant.

"*How?*" demanded an Indian merchant.

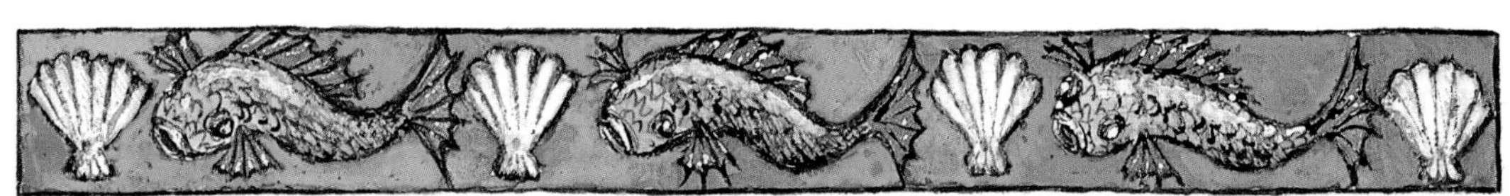

"*When?*" cried a Venetian merchant.

"Now!" answered Sadko. "I wager that I'll catch the fish tonight, or work for each of you without pay for the rest of my life!"

"I have a magnificent ship, far from here, upon the open sea. It's yours if you can catch these golden fish," roared the Viking.

"My ship too," chuckled the Indian.

"And mine!" laughed the Venetian.

They followed Sadko to the shores of Lake Ilmen and watched him cast his net onto the silver surface of the water.

"Where are your fairy-tale fish, Minstrel?" shouted Vladimir.

Sadko said nothing and left his nets there a little longer. The three foreign merchants began to think of the hardest work they could find for Sadko. But as he pulled his nets in, they all saw something that took the breath from their mouths. There, in Sadko's nets, lay the three fish promised by the Princess Volkova, each with fins of gold!

Sadko returned to Novgorod no mere minstrel. Now he was a merchant too, with three fine ships to sail across the blue ocean. He started at once to buy and sell rich wares from the edges of the world and was soon the wealthiest fellow in the city. He bought a fine house and promised to marry Lubasha, the prettiest of girls. But Novgorod was such a long, dusty journey from the sea that Sadko saw less and less of Lubasha. He traveled back and forth across the ocean many times in a year, always raising his goblet to toast the health of the Tsar of the Sea, to be sure he enjoyed fair weather and a safe journey.

"Hail to the noble Tsar of the Sea,
I raise my cup and drink to thee!"

he would say, and he grew to like the life he had at sea.

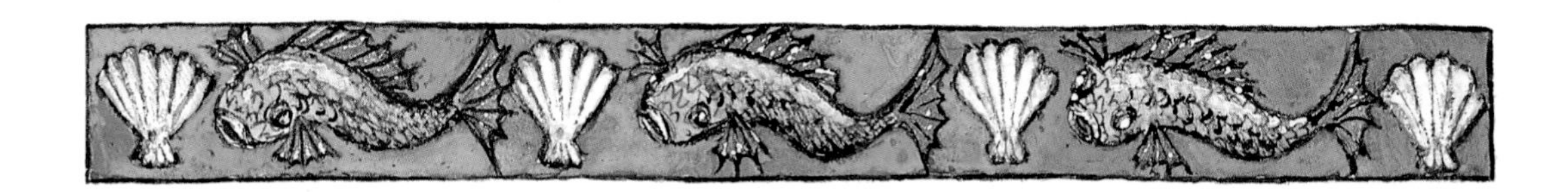

Then one day, as Sadko's three ships traveled once more upon the sparkling water, a squall came down and threw the ships this way and that like leaves upon a breeze. The Tsar of the Sea was angry, for Sadko had forgotten to raise a goblet to his health.

The wind howled like Baba-Yaga's cry, and the seas churned like her boiling caldron. Desperate to save his valuable fleet from destruction, Sadko had his men lift up caskets of jewels and throw them into the foaming waves as a gift for the Sea Tsar.

At once the storm subsided. The sun burst out and the sea lay before them like a mirror. But something was wrong. The sails hung like damp linen, and not a breath of wind came across the water to fill them. There they stayed, as still as if on dry land.

The sailors saw they were becalmed and reasoned that someone among them must be a jinx. In order to reveal him they decided that each should cast a button into the sea. He whose button sank first would be the one who had brought the bad luck upon them.

One by one they ripped a silver button from their shirts and tossed it upon the surface of the water. The buttons bounced as if they had been thrown onto dry land. Last of all, Sadko tore off his button, which was wooden, and threw it upon the water. No sooner had it touched the surface than it sank out of sight.

Sadko was a noble fellow, and in order to save the other sailors he jumped over the rail of the ship into the sea, with his goosli under his arm. Then, as the wind came gently across the water, filling the sails, the three ships sailed off and out of sight.

The goosli kept Sadko afloat, but he began to grow tired. Then suddenly, something pulled at his ankle! And again! A great hand grabbed at his leg, pulling him under the sea. Fighting for breath, Sadko saw the blurred shape of a slimy, scaly sea monster, dragging him down, down, down....

The sun could not reach the bed of the ocean, but something was glowing brightly ahead of them. It was a palace, made of pearls and diamonds, silver and gold, and treasures from a thousand shipwrecks. And inside, upon a magnificent throne, sat the Tsar of the Sea surrounded by his thirty beautiful daughters. The youngest of them all smiled broadly at Sadko. It was the Princess Volkova from Lake Ilmen. It was she who had persuaded her father to becalm the stormy sea. Had it not been for her, the Tsar of the Sea would certainly have drowned Sadko.

"Greetings, Minstrel," boomed the Tsar. "How splendid that you have come in person to wish me good health!" The Tsar roared with laughter.

"Make him sing," said Volkova to her father.

The Tsar leaned toward Sadko. "I hear that you play well upon your goosli, and I wish you to entertain us."

Sadko picked up his goosli with a shaking hand, and played the most cheerful song he could remember. The thirty daughters of the Tsar swayed and sighed to the music, and when it was finished the Tsar clapped his great scaly hands and said:

"Minstrel, that was most diverting, and for your reward you may choose one of my daughters as your bride."

Sadko did not dare refuse, even though he loved Lubasha.

The thirty sea princesses drifted past, each lovelier than the one before. But it was the very last, his own sweet water sprite, that he chose.

"Let us celebrate the match!" bellowed the Tsar of the Sea. "I command you to play, Sadko, play like never before!"

Thus commanded, Sadko took up his goosli and began.

At first he played slowly, and his pretty fiancée swayed elegantly in front of him singing softly, like water trickling in a stream.

Then he played faster, beating a rhythm with his foot. Faster and faster went the song, and the mermaids danced and the sea monsters swam.

The princesses sang, and the sea horses pranced around and around in a great swirl. And still Sadko played faster, and still faster than that, for he found that he could not stop. The water throbbed and shook with the rhythms of the music. Onward they danced, all the fish and the crabs, the lobsters and jellyfish, moonfish, starfish, and all!

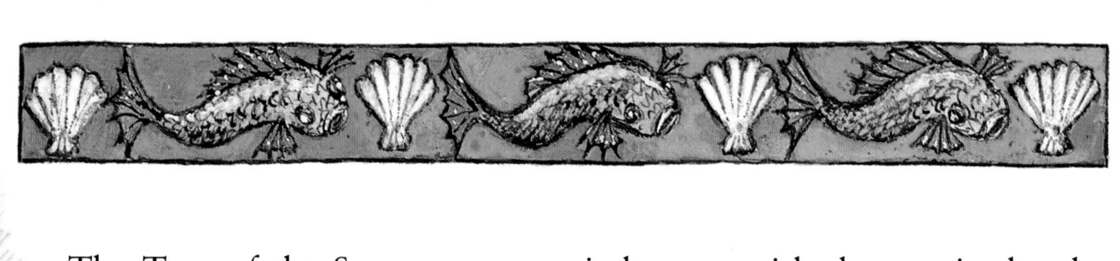

The Tsar of the Sea was so carried away with the music that he got up off his throne and began to dance as well, faster and faster until the Ocean herself was dancing.

A terrible storm raged above them, for their dancing sent great waves crashing across the sea, and still they danced, and still Sadko played. He could not stop, not even when he heard the howling of the storm, nor when he saw his own fleet of ships being driven toward the rocks.

Then he saw a shining figure walking toward him, a figure of golden light. It held up a hand and said, "Sadko, stop your playing, or your fellow merchants will drown."

"But I cannot stop," cried Sadko, "for I am under the command of the Tsar of the Sea."

"Listen to me," shouted the figure through the violent water. "You must break the strings and tear out the pegs of your goosli, for no one will harm a sailor who is with his patron saint!"

"Saint Nikolai of Mozhaysk!" shouted Sadko. He threw down his beautiful goosli and smashed it into a thousand pieces.

The sea creatures stopped their wild dancing, and the sea became still.

"Now go home, Sadko!" said Saint Nikolai. "Go back to the fair city of Novgorod, for your good fortune upon the sea is over."

Little Volkova wept, for she could not bear to be parted from Sadko. And as Saint Nikolai led him to the shore of Lake Ilmen, she swam after them, singing her sad song like trickling water in a stream.

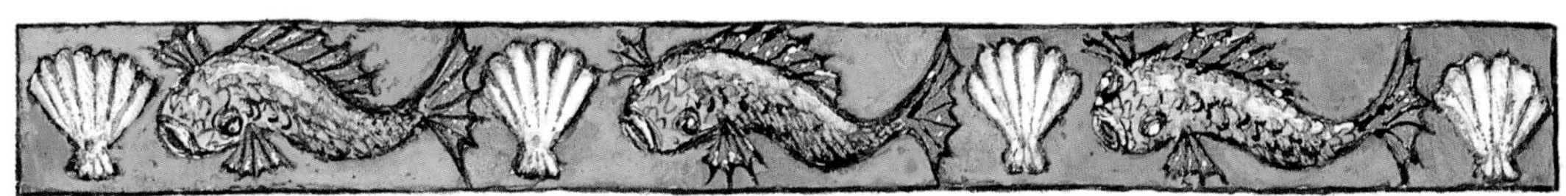

"You cannot live among people," Saint Nikolai said to her. "You must stay in the sea where you belong."

"But then I should never hear Sadko sing again!" she wept. "Is there no way for me to be near him?"

Saint Nikolai took pity on her, for he knew it was she who had saved Sadko's life.

"You will live on both land and sea, fair Volkova," he said. And raising his hands, he transformed her into a broad, shining river that flowed all the way from Novgorod to the ocean. As it flowed by him, Sadko heard what sounded like the song of the Sea Tsar's youngest daughter.

Sadko promised himself there and then to sing to her as often as he could, so that she would not be lonely, for he could never forget that but for her he would surely have drowned.

All Novgorod rejoiced, for it is not every day that a new river flows by a town and turns it from an ordinary market into a fine port. And what should sail into the harbor first? None other than Sadko's three ships.

"Greetings, Sadko! We are much relieved to see you survived those terrible storms!" shouted the sailors. "Tell us, which river has carried us to Novgorod?"

"Well, my friends," said Sadko, thinking of the sea princess, "this is the river Volkova, and she is the loveliest river in all Russia!"

Without another word he rushed off through the gates of Novgorod to find his pretty Lubasha. You can imagine how pleased she was to have her handsome Sadko home again, safe and well.

"Dear Lubasha," said Sadko, embracing his beloved, "do not let me leave you alone again."

"Of course not, my minstrel," she replied. "But I was never

alone, for your songs are in my heart and you were always in my prayers."

Hearing this, Sadko went to the harbor and sold his three ships and never once went to sea again. He used the money to build a great cathedral in the name of Saint Nikolai of Mozhaysk, patron saint of all sailors. On the very day it was finished he married his good and kind Lubasha. With the few rubles that were left he bought a maple tree. He felled the tree and from the wood carved the finest goosli you ever saw.

Every fine summer evening Sadko kept his promise to Volkova. He would sit by the river with Lubasha, singing and playing his goosli.

"Sing me the song of the sea princess once more," Lubasha would say to him.

"Once more then, my love," he would answer. "Once more."

And beside them, the river Volkova sang along, the happy laughing sound of water trickling in a stream.

III
Tsar Saltan and Koshka the Cat

KOSHKA YAWNED, showing all her teeth. "I'm glad that's over. I don't like to think about all that water," she said.

"Well, I liked the tale," said the old merchant. "I shall always remember to say a toast to the Tsar of the Sea."

"Will you tell Tsar Saltan about our friend?" asked Militrissa.

"Good lady, we shall tell the tsar all we have heard here, and I am sure he will accept your kind invitation without delay."

"We shall see," said Militrissa, and together with Guidon she bade farewell to the merchants.

Across the seven seas and beyond the thrice-nine lands the merchants sailed, and when they were halfway, they each filled a goblet with mead and shouted:

"Hail to the noble Tsar of the Sea,
We raise our cups and we drink to thee!"

A fair wind filled the sails and swept them forward to the realm of Tsar Saltan Saltanovich the Magnificent. They greeted the tsar and presented him with the wines and meads they had brought, and Saltan was most pleased. There was a great feast in honor of the merchants. The royal musicians sang, and the royal storytellers spoke, and all in the palace came to hear them. The tsar sat at the

head of the great oak table with Katooshka and Liza Poffarikha on either side.

"Tell me," said the tsar to the old merchant, "did you find the Island of Bouyan, with the mighty oak tree upon a hill?"

"It was where we left it, Sire, with the lady and her son, still listening to the tales of the enchanted cat."

"But did the cat know the tale of Sadko?" asked the tsar.

"Oh yes, Great Tsar, and it was worth asking to hear," said the old merchant, and he told him the tale of Sadko.

"Truly I have never heard a story to equal it, not even from my own storytellers!" said the tsar. "I too shall hear a story from this cat. Pack my bags and prepare to set sail."

Well, the two horrid sisters had gaped and gasped throughout the story, and at last they slipped out of the room in a panic.

"What now?" whispered Liza Poffarikha.

"We'll ask old Baba-Yaga," said Katooshka. "This was her idea, after all."

They dashed through the forest, fighting their way past the thorny trees until at last they reached Baba-Yaga's hut.

"Granny, let us in!" said Katooshka.

"The tsar sets sail for the Island of Bouyan tonight!" squeaked Liza Poffarikha.

Baba-Yaga was in a cheerful mood for once and laughed at them. "Ha! You think it's a problem, do you? Well, I could say I was going to eat you, but instead I shall tell you what to do. Tell the tsar to ask the merchants if the cat knows the story of the Firebird, Tsarevich Ivan, and Gray Wolf. This is a tale of much power, a greater tale than the one before. And it is a tale only I know. Now go away, because I might be hungry soon and who knows what I might want to eat!"

The sisters fled, and when they reached the palace, they found the tsar with his luggage, about to leave.

"My lord!" said Katooshka. "Where are you going? Surely not to this island called Bouyan?"

"I cannot believe a word the merchants say," said Liza Poffarikha. "But even if it is true, is it really so wonderful?"

"Can you think of anything more wonderful than a cat who tells good stories?" said the tsar.

"Well, can you be sure the cat knows any others?" said the elder sister. "If, however, the cat were to know the story of the Firebird, Tsarevich Ivan, and Gray Wolf, it would be a wonder indeed."

"Otherwise, I'd say it was a very ordinary cat," said the other sister. "Perhaps you should command the merchants to find out for you, for it is a long way to go to find out yourself."

The tsar saw sense in what they told him and had his bags unpacked. He called his storytellers to him and asked them to tell him the tale of the Firebird. None had heard of it, so the tsar commanded the merchants to ask the cat to tell the story of the Firebird. They agreed and set sail there and then.

Time passed. After sailing beyond the thrice-nine realms and across the seven seas, the merchants were again returning from their voyage and were bound for Tsar Saltan's realm, when they came upon the Isle of Bouyan. They lowered their anchor in the bay and came ashore, where Militrissa and Guidon greeted them.

"Welcome again," said Militrissa. "How was your trip?"

"We have been lucky, good lady," said the old merchant. "But then we always remember to toast the Tsar of the Sea."

"I am glad you remembered Koshka's tale," said Guidon. "But did you remember to tell Tsar Saltan that the cat told it to you?"

"We told him, but he seemed to think another tale was needed

from the cat before he considered it a wonder worth visiting."

"If I came with you, I could tell the tsar that this cat is a wonder," said Guidon.

"Alas, the ship is brimming with the finest timbers from around the world, and a single matchstick more would surely sink and drown us all," said the merchant.

"It matters not," said Militrissa, "for we have not been invited there in any case. Come up the hill and see if the cat knows the tale you wish to hear."

They found Koshka sleeping, as usual. "Back already?" she said, yawning. "What is it this time? A nice little song? I know some good tunes!" And she hopped to the right and began caterwauling.

The merchants, young and old, covered their ears, and Militrissa said, "Dearest kitty, we'd prefer a story!"

"Very well," sighed the cat. "I daresay you will let me sing one day. But tell me, which story do you want to hear?"

"There is a story, which none of us knows, about a Firebird," said the old merchant. "We would all like to hear it."

"Oh, that's one of my best stories," said Koshka, scratching her ear. "Now then, how does it start? Oh yes, I remember, it starts in a garden."

"A garden?" said Militrissa.

"A garden unlike any you have ever seen," said Koshka. "Now be quiet all of you and listen, for this is a tale worth hearing."

And seeing everyone was silent, Koshka folded her paws under her and began to speak.

The Firebird, Ivan, and Gray Wolf

Imagine a garden where each flower and tree was made of jewels or precious stones. The shrubs had emerald leaves. Diamonds grew there and silver roses. Their equal could not be found in any tsardom in Russia. But the rarest tree of all was just a rather small, simple apple tree, for each autumn this tree bore fruit of gold.

This was the garden of Tsar Dadon, and naturally he watched over it with a keen eye. He was especially careful with the apple tree, for its fruits were dearer to him than any other jewel in his enchanted garden. That is why, one morning, he noticed that a golden apple had been stolen during the night.

Now, the tsar trusted no one except his three sons, Dmitri, Fyodor, and Ivan. He called them to his throne room and told them, in a whisper, about the theft.

"Whichever one of you catches the nighttime thief can have half of my tsardom," he said.

"I am the eldest, let me catch the thief," said Dmitri. He badly wanted half of his father's valuable tsardom.

All night long he sat by the tree and waited for the thief. But no one came, and the glistening garden of riches was silent. Finally, Dmitri saw a glow in the sky, toward the east.

"At last! It is morning," he sighed, and believing the tree to be safe, he allowed his eyes to close for a single moment. But when he opened them again, the sky was black once more. And when he looked at the magical tree he saw that an apple had been taken.

The Tsar's second son, Fyodor, was also eager to gain half his father's tsardom. The next night he sat by the tree determined to remain awake. Just as it seemed he could no longer do so, he saw a warm glow on the eastern horizon.

"Thank goodness! It is morning," said Fyodor, and he allowed his eyes to close for half a moment. But when he opened them it was dark night again and another apple had gone.

Ivan, the Tsar's youngest son, cared little for half of the tsardom but wanted to set his beloved father's mind at rest.

So the next night Ivan sat by the apple tree and fought against the sleep that pressed down on him like a heavy blanket. And so strong willed was he that he did not close his eyes once, not even when the sky grew pale in the east.

But it was not the sun that made the heavens catch fire. Across the sky, like a comet, came the Firebird. Glowing brightly, she settled on the magic tree and began to eat a golden apple.

Quickly, quietly, Ivan stole up behind the fabulous creature, stretched on his toes, and took hold of the Firebird's tail. It burned! But Ivan was brave and he held his grip.

"Please do not harm me, Tsarevich!" cried the Firebird, and as she flew upward, a single feather fell from her tail into Ivan's scorched hand. It no longer burned but flashed and glowed all shades of gold in the first brightness of dawn.

"Take this feather in exchange for the apples," said the Firebird. "If I ever take it back, I will serve you with my life."

Then the Firebird spread her glorious burning wings and flew out of sight.

Ivan ran off at once to show the Firebird's gift to the tsar. The tsar, however, decided that the feather was not enough. "I must have this fabulous creature," he said. "She will be my prisoner, for taking the golden apples."

But the Firebird never returned to the tsar's garden. However many nights the three tsarevich-princes sat and watched, they never saw the bird again. The tsar could neither eat nor sleep. "You shall have half of my tsardom if you can find the Firebird," he said to his three sons.

Dmitri, jealous of Ivan's success, set off at once, determined to win half the tsardom. But when, after a month, he failed to return, Fyodor went in search of the magical bird, for he was as greedy as Dmitri and just as jealous of Ivan.

Another month passed, but neither brother returned. So Ivan took it upon himself to follow his brothers, despite the pleas of his father, who thought he was too young.

"Go if you must," said the tsar, "but take the Firebird's feather and place it in your cap. May it bring you good fortune."

Ivan saddled up his horse and set off. He soon reached a crossroads where a notice read: "Go back and fail, go forward and starve, go left and be eaten by wolves, go right and your horse will be eaten."

Ivan rode ahead, unafraid of hunger. But his horse was a noble animal, which turned around and galloped to the right.

No sooner had the horse done so than a large gray wolf leaped out of the forest and attacked and ate Ivan's horse.

For three days and nights the young tsarevich wept over the bones of his trusted companion. Finally, Gray Wolf took pity on Ivan, stole up, and licked his face.

"Can I not ease your sorrow, for it was I who caused it?"

"Alas, my horse is gone, and I have no way of finding the Firebird, which my father, Tsar Dadon, pines for."

"Then climb upon my back, for I know where to find the Firebird," said the wolf. "I am strong and can carry you and will be your faithful servant." Ivan did as he was told, and Gray Wolf raced off at a great speed.

The high mountains and deep blue lakes, green forests and golden cities of old Mother Russia raced by, for the wolf all but flew. Whether or not it was a long time, who knows? For a deed takes time, but a tale is quickly told. At last they stopped in front of the great palace of Tsar Afron, which was surrounded by a high wall.

"Beyond the wall you will find the Firebird in a jeweled cage," said Gray Wolf. "Take the bird, but leave the cage."

Ivan stood on the wolf's back, climbed the wall, and jumped into a garden on the other side. It was full of light, for at the very center, in a magnificent cage, was the Firebird. Ivan was about to take the bird when he remembered how he had burned his hand and thought, "Surely if I can take the bird without being seen, I can take her cage too." So he carefully lifted the cage down from where it hung.

All at once the bells in the palace towers rang out, for the cage was tied to them by a thousand invisible threads. Guards appeared

as if from nowhere, and they dragged Ivan to Tsar Afron.

"You are an unlikely thief," bellowed the tsar, who could see Ivan was a nobleman. "Explain yourself!"

"Sire, I am the son of Tsar Dadon, and I took the bird because she stole my father's golden apples," said Ivan.

"Had you come to me with your father's name to ask for the bird I should have given her to you, but to steal her and her cage is a severe crime," said Afron. "I understand well your father's sadness, for my horse of power, Chestnut-Gray, was taken by Tsar Berendey, and I long for this great animal to be mine again."

"Allow me to clear my name by returning this horse to you," said Ivan.

"Very well. Do so and I will pardon you," said Afron. "Leave at once, and take the Firebird and her cage. They are yours now, but whether as a prince or as a common thief is up to you."

Ivan took the cage and climbed back over the wall. With shame, Ivan told Gray Wolf all that had happened.

"Young master, why could you not use your handkerchief to stop your hand from burning?" sighed the wolf. "I can help you, though, so climb on."

Ivan held onto Gray Wolf's thick fur, and they galloped off again to the tsardom beyond, over mountains, across lakes, through forests, and around cities. It seemed like no time at all before they were outside the high wall of Tsar Berendey's palace.

"Over the wall are Berendey's stables," said Gray Wolf. "There, you will find Chestnut-Gray, Tsar Afron's horse of power. Take the horse, but do not touch his bridle."

Gray Wolf allowed Ivan to climb on his back to get over the wall. He ran quickly to the stables and found the horse of power, which had a golden mane, silver hooves, and a bridle of priceless jewels.

"How will I control such a beast with no bridle?" thought Ivan. So he gently loosened the reins and took the horse and bridle together.

No sooner had he done so than every single bell in Tsar Berendey's palace rang out, for the bridle was joined to them by a thousand invisible threads. Hidden guards jumped upon Ivan and threw him before Tsar Berendey.

"You robbed me of my horse and bridle," shouted the tsar, who could see Ivan was a prince. "Explain yourself!"

"Forgive me, Sire, I stole Chestnut-Gray for Tsar Afron who pines for the horse of power that belongs to him."

"I understand Afron's misery, for my own daughter, the Princess of Inexhaustible Loveliness, was stolen many years ago," said Berendey sadly. But then he grew angry again. "Had you come to me with Afron's request I would have given you the horse, for it is indeed his. But the bridle is mine, and therefore the crime is severe."

"Allow me to clear my name, Great Tsar," said Ivan. "I will recapture your beloved daughter and return her safely to you."

"Young Tsarevich, do this and you will be rewarded with her hand in marriage. Yet I fear it is impossible, for she is the prisoner of Kastchey-the-Deathless, the sorcerer of the dead. He is thousands of years old, for his death is hidden. No one knows where he keeps it and because of this he cannot die."

"Then I will find his death and defeat him in order to return your daughter to you," said Ivan.

"Take the horse of power and his bridle; they are yours," said Tsar Berendey. "But whether as a prince or a common thief is now up to you."

Ivan took the horse of power to where Gray Wolf and the Firebird were waiting. Red-faced, Ivan related the whole story.

"Foolish Tsarevich," sighed Gray Wolf. "You should have used your belt to harness the horse. But do not worry, I can help you. Climb on my back and hold tight."

Ivan did what Gray Wolf told him, and holding the cage of the Firebird and the bridle of Chestnut-Gray, they set off once more. Through the next tsardom and beyond Gray Wolf raced, and it was a good thing that Chestnut-Gray was a horse of power, or he would surely have been left behind.

At length it began to grow dark, and it was soon darker than midnight. Fortunately, the Firebird lit the way, so Ivan soon saw that they had reached Kastchey's evil realm.

"You must go on alone, young Tsarevich," said Gray Wolf sadly. "Take the princess, but leave her silver and golden slippers."

Inside a castle, in a tall tower, slept the Princess of Inexhaustible Loveliness. So lovely was she that although the castle was hung with a thousand mirrors, none could show all her beauty at once because there was so much of it.

Every day she searched for her captor's death.

"Perhaps my death is in the broom by the door," Kastchey would say. But when the princess broke the broom, she knew it was not there, for the sorcerer did not die.

"Perhaps it is in an egg," he would say, so the princess had eggs for breakfast. But still the old wizard lived.

"Perhaps it is in my daughter's tears," Kastchey said.

But Kastchevna, his daughter, had never shed a tear in all her life, for though she was beautiful, her heart was made of wood.

Ivan quickly climbed the vines that clung to the tower, slipped through a window, and found the Princess of Inexhaustible Loveliness asleep on a great bed. She awoke at once, but when she saw Ivan she was not afraid, for he had a kind face.

She was indeed lovely, and Ivan fell in love with her the moment he saw her.

"Quickly, your Loveliness," he whispered. "We must not delay." He carried her to the window and told her to hold onto him as he climbed back down the vine. But the princess was wearing her silver and golden slippers, and all the alarms in Kastchey's castle rang out, for the slippers had been attached to them by a thousand invisible threads. Kastchey and Kastchevna ran outside and waited at the bottom of the tower.

"Thief!" squealed Kastchey, when Ivan and the Princess reached the ground. "How dare you take what is mine?"

But by the light of the Firebird's feather Kastchevna saw Ivan's handsome face, and she felt a green shoot bursting out of her wooden heart.

"Father, do not harm the prince," she said.

Kastchey was most surprised, but he saw that his daughter had fallen in love with Ivan, so he said, "If the prince will stay by his own choice, the princess can go free."

Ivan knew not what to say, for he loved the princess and wanted to free her, yet could not bear to be parted from her. The princess herself spoke before he could. "Ivan cannot stay, for I love him and only death can part us!"

Kastchevna looked so disappointed that the Princess Loveliness was filled with pity for her. She stepped forward and kissed her on

the forehead. Kastchevna's wooden heart split in two. She covered her face with her hands and wept, great tears splashing on the earth. Then roots shot out of her shoes, branches from her sleeves, until the tears fell not from Kastchevna but from the leaves of the weeping willow tree she had become.

"My death!" screamed Kastchey, for it really was hidden in his daughter's tears, and he crumbled like a dry leaf before their eyes. His cry was so loud it was heard by Tsar Berendey and Tsar Afron and Tsar Dadon, so many tsardoms away.

Ivan took the princess by the hand, and together they pushed open the great rusty gates of Kastchey's realm and ran out into the sunshine beyond.

Then they climbed upon Gray Wolf, one holding the Firebird's cage, one holding the bridle of Chestnut-Gray. And they set off at such a pace that within a day they had arrived at Tsar Berendey's palace.

The tsar had never known such happiness. "Tsarevich, you have cleared your name with me. Chestnut-Gray and his bridle are yours as a prince, and my beloved daughter, Loveliness, shall be your bride tomorrow morning."

So the next day Ivan married the Princess of Inexhaustible Loveliness. As soon as the feasting was over the two of them climbed upon Gray Wolf and set off with Chestnut-Gray and the Firebird for the realm of Tsar Afron. Back across the forests and lakes they flew, past cities and over mountains, and by nightfall they had put Chestnut Gray back in Tsar Afron's stable.

"You have cleared your name, Tsarevich," said the delighted tsar. "Take the Firebird and her cage, they are yours as a prince!"

And so Ivan, the princess, and the Firebird set off upon Gray Wolf once more, to the end of the tsardom and across the thrice-

nine realms. All too soon, Gray Wolf came to the crossroads where he had eaten Ivan's horse.

"I leave you here, little master, for I have repaid my debt."

So Ivan embraced his friend, and then he set off with his beautiful bride and the Firebird for the long walk to his father's palace. But along the road they encountered two noblemen on horseback. At first Ivan could not see who they were, but as he got closer he saw it was his own two brothers, Dmitri and Fyodor, returning from their unsuccessful quest.

"Ivan has captured the Firebird," hissed Dmitri.

"And he has taken a wife of breathtaking loveliness," growled Fyodor. They both boiled with jealousy, and as Ivan embraced them, they stuck their knives into his heart and carried off the princess and the Firebird.

For three days Ivan lay dead by the roadside, while his brothers were welcomed by Tsar Dadon as heroes. Dmitri took half his father's tsardom, and Fyodor decided to take the princess for his wife. The princess had been struck dumb by the sight of her beloved's death and so could not tell the tsar the truth.

But on the night of the third day, Gray Wolf saw something glowing at the side of the road. It was the feather of the Firebird, still in Ivan's cap. Seeing the fate that had befallen his dearest friend, Gray Wolf lay down beside him and wept. All at once the sky was filled with a brilliant light. The Princess Loveliness could not speak herself, but she could free the Firebird and had done so. The Firebird flew to where Gray Wolf and Ivan lay. She took the feather from Ivan's cap and said:

"Weep not, Gray Wolf, this feather gives me the strength

to serve our friend. I will fly to the ends of the earth to find the Water of Life, but I must hurry, for Tsarevich Fyodor marries the Princess Loveliness in the morning."

With that, she flew off like a spark from a chimney across the black sky.

Whether it was a long time or not, who knows? For a deed takes time, but this tale is nearly told. The Firebird reached the ends of the earth, where a clear stream ran from a spring in the ground. As she filled her beak, the stream said, "If I give you a life, you will owe me a life."

"Then I shall give you mine," said the Firebird, knowing she had found the Water of Life. Quickly she flew back to the other side of the world to where Gray Wolf had waited patiently. The Firebird sprinkled the water of life onto Ivan. This done, she lay down upon the ground and died.

Ivan opened his eyes and said, "My goodness, how well I have slept!"

"But for the Firebird you would never have awoken," said Gray Wolf.

Ivan looked down at where the Firebird lay. She no longer burned; her feathers were cold and ashen.

"Who did this to you, my noble creature?" he cried.

Then he saw the feather was gone from his cap, and he remembered the Firebird's promise to serve him with her life. Tenderly he lifted her off the ground and sobbed with grief.

"We must hurry, Prince," said Gray Wolf. "Your brother Fyodor weds your wife today."

Already the sun had risen in the sky. Ivan set off upon Gray Wolf with the Firebird held gently in his arms. They burst in upon the ceremony just as Fyodor was about to place a ring on the princess's

finger. Her face was wet with tears, but the instant she saw her beloved Ivan her voice came back.

"Thieves! Villains!" she cried, pointing in turn to Dmitri and Fyodor, and she told the tsar the true story.

The tsar cast his two eldest sons onto the ground. "May you be known across the thrice-nine lands and beyond as common thieves!" he bellowed. "For you are no longer sons of mine!" And the two of them fled from Dadon's realm, never to return.

That evening Ivan built a fire and placed the Firebird in the flames. When the last feather had burned, there appeared in the ashes a golden egg. It split in half and out flew the Firebird, reborn, brighter, and more beautiful than ever before!

The tsar was so grateful to her that he allowed her to come and go from his garden at will and to eat from his tree of golden apples whenever she wanted.

For each apple she ate, she left a seed, and from each seed grew another tree. They were ordinary, simple apple trees, but every autumn they bore fruit of gold!

IV

Tsar Saltan and Koshka the Cat

"I HOPE YOU ENJOYED the tale, for there are plenty more like it!" said Koshka. "Do I deserve a small fish for my trouble?"

"No, you deserve a big fish, clever cat!" said Guidon. "I'll catch you one right away." As soon as he had done so, he returned and baked the fish, and Koshka shared it with them all.

"It is time to cast off, my lady," said the merchant, as he finished his piece of fish. "For I must not miss the tide."

"Send our greetings once more to Tsar Saltan," said Militrissa. "Tell him all you saw and heard, kind friend."

"We shall not forget such a tale in a hurry," said the merchant. "The tsar will surely hasten to come when he hears of it."

And with that, the merchants returned to their ship and sailed once more to the east across the seven seas and beyond the thrice-nine lands to the realm of Tsar Saltan Saltanovich the Magnificent, pausing only to fill their goblets and say:

"Hail to the noble Tsar of the Sea,
We raise our cups and we drink to thee!"

So they arrived safe and well, and Tsar Saltan greeted them with a great banquet. Then the time came for the old merchant to tell the

tale of his travels, and none of the guests listened harder than Katooshka and Liza Poffarikha.

"My friend," said the tsar to the old merchant, "did you perchance encounter the Isle of Bouyan this time?"

"It was where we left it, great Tsar," said the old merchant, "and the lady with her son are still awaiting you and continue to pass time with the storytelling cat."

"But did the cat know the tale of the Firebird?"

"She knew the tale from beginning to end," said the old merchant. "It is a tale to make your eyes bulge and your ears ring!" And he recounted the tale there and then.

Katooshka and Liza Poffarikha sat there with their eyes bulging and their ears ringing, unable to believe what they had heard.

"My word," said the tsar. "That's a tale of wonder indeed!"

"And the cat knows many others," said the old merchant.

"Then I shall set sail tonight," said the tsar, and he ordered his bags to be packed and his ship to be made ready for sailing.

Katooshka and Liza Poffarikha left the palace at once and dashed through the forest, this way and that, barely pausing for breath until they had reached Baba-Yaga's hut.

Old Bony-Legs poked her head out of the window. "Greetings, little children!" she said. She had smelled them a mile off and licked her lips, for she planned to eat them. She had put a pan of sauce on the fire and set her table.

"Granny, we are all lost," wept Katooshka.

"The tsar sails tonight for the Island of Bouyan," wailed Liza Poffarikha. "The tale of the Firebird has been told!"

Baba-Yaga flung open her door. "Impossible!" she screeched.

But after the two sisters had related the tale to her, she jumped up and down and pulled at her ashen hair, squealing and shouting.

"Well it was all your idea in the first place," said Katooshka. "So what's to be done?"

"Well I'll tell you! If you speak to Baba-Yaga like that you get eaten — that's what is to be done!"

"Do not eat my foolish sister," said Liza Poffarikha. "She's all skin and bone."

"Shall I eat you instead?" said the witch, teasing her.

"Oh no, Granny, I'm sure I would give you a stomachache!"

"Well, you'd better come in while I think," said the witch.

The gates of bones swung open, and the two sisters stepped cautiously into the witch's hut. Baba-Yaga stirred the contents of a pot, burning away in the hearth.

"Completely spoiled," she said glumly. "All your fault!" She decided not to eat the sisters today, after all, since she had lost her appetite. "Now why I should help two silly little girls like you I can't imagine, but there is one story, the most powerful, dangerous story of them all, and truly, no one but I can know of it."

"What is it called?" said Katooshka, barely breathing.

"Tell us, Babooshka," squeaked Liza Poffarikha.

"It is my own tale!" said the witch, her eyes shining. "The tale of Baba-Yaga and a girl named Vassilisa."

"We shall tell the tsar to command the merchants to ask the cat to tell this tale," giggled the sisters. "And when the cat fails, the tsar will cast that old merchant into the sea."

"Well, go off quickly before I get hungry again," said Baba-Yaga, and she shoved them out of her hut.

The sisters said not a word as they sped through the dark forest. They found the tsar on his way to the ship, before they even reached the palace.

"The story of the Firebird is not so wonderful," sighed

Katooshka, "for I have heard that there is a tale much more splendid, and it is so powerful no one knows it."

"But if the cat knows the tale, she is a wonder indeed, and will certainly know other tales," said Liza Poffarikha.

"And what is this tale about?" asked the tsar.

"It is about the witch Baba-Yaga!" said Katooshka.

"And a maiden named Vassilisa!" said Liza Poffarikha.

The tsar stroked his beard. "Why, I have heard that a terrible witch by this name lives within my own realm. I should like to hear this story very much!" And he summoned his storytellers and asked them about Baba-Yaga the witch. Yet not one of them knew her tale. The tsar grew angry. "I must hear this story. I shall go at once to the Isle of Bouyan to ask the cat!"

"The cat may not know it," said Liza Poffarikha.

"Then I shall search my whole tsardom and beyond for a storyteller who does," said the tsar.

"You could command the merchant to find such a storyteller for you," said Katooshka.

"Yes!" said the tsar. "You are right." He commanded the old merchant to sail the seven seas and search beyond the thrice-nine realms until he had heard the tale of the witch Baba-Yaga.

Right away the merchants set sail. Beyond the thrice-nine realms and across the seven seas they went, and at every port they asked to hear the tale of Baba-Yaga and Vassilisa. The greatest storytellers of each land were brought forth, but no one knew the tale. At last the merchants came upon the Isle of Bouyan.

"Greetings, our friends! Have you brought Tsar Saltan?" shouted Guidon from the grassy hilltop.

"No, young lad!" replied the merchant, lowering the anchor. He came ashore and told Guidon and Militrissa the tsar's request.

"Baba-Yaga lives in Saltan's own realm, so they say," said the old merchant. "Why, no one knows what she does deep in the forest there, so how can the cat know this tale?"

"We must ask her, Sir," said Guidon, "for I don't suppose there is room for me upon your fair ship?"

"No, lad," he said. "We are weighed down with foods for Tsar Saltan. Another morsel and we would surely all sink and drown."

"Then we will ask Koshka to tell us this tale," said Militrissa.

Koshka was waiting for them, for she enjoyed her tale-telling afternoons. "Well, what tale is it today?" she said, pacing left and right. "Happy or sad, funny or not?"

"We want to hear about the witch Baba-Yaga," said Guidon.

Koshka arched her back, hissed, and spat. "Why this tale?" she demanded.

"It is the tale Tsar Saltan requested, dearest," said Militrissa. "Do you not know it?"

"I know the tale," said Koshka. "But it is not one I care to tell."

"Oh please, dear, kind, clever Koshka," said Guidon. "I will catch you a specially big and tasty fish!"

"Well..." mumbled the old black cat. "It will have to be a *very* big fish."

"It will be," said Guidon. "The biggest, tastiest fish you ever ate."

"All right then," said Koshka, walking around the tree to the left. "But listen hard, because I'll tell this tale only once!"

Everyone sat down and listened as hard as they could, as Koshka opened her wide green eyes and began.

Vassilisa the Fair and Baba-Yaga

In a certain tsardom, in a certain realm, there lived a blacksmith and his wife. They had the prettiest daughter in the village. She was not only beautiful, but kind and warmhearted, too, and it is not often you find all these things in one person. They called her Vassilisa the Fair, and they loved her dearly.

But sad things happen even to good folk, and one day Vassilisa's mother became ill. She called her daughter to her bedside and gave her a little doll. Inside the doll was a second doll, and inside that was a third doll called Kookolka, and she was so small that Vassilisa barely dared to hold her. Her mother said to her, "Whenever you need help, feed little Kookolka and say:

'Eat up quickly, little one,
Then tell me, please, what should be done!' "

Then Vassilisa's mother died, and the blacksmith and his daughter wept for many days and nights. But time heals, and before long the blacksmith found himself another wife. She was a widow, who already had two daughters, and because of this the blacksmith thought she would make a good mother for Vassilisa. But she did not have enough love in her heart for three children and was kind only to her own.

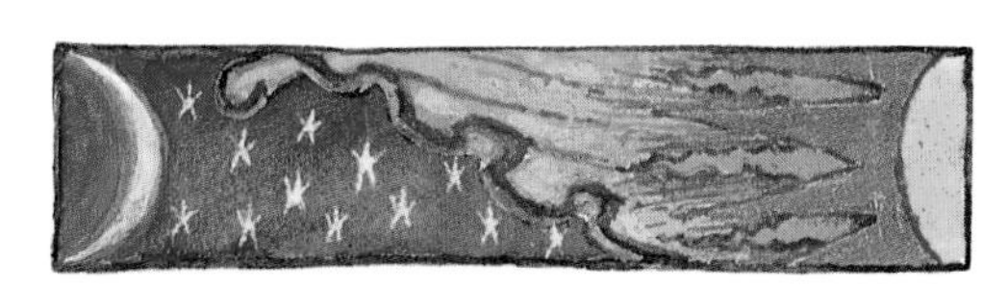

She dressed Vassilisa in rags, but bought silk for her own daughters. They ate like tsaritsas every day, while the stepmother gave Vassilisa barely enough food to feed a sparrow. Yet the sisters looked quite plain next to Vassilisa the Fair, so they sent her out in all weathers on errands, hoping the snow and rain would wash away her beauty, or that the sun would dry it up.

But Vassilisa took the doll that her mother had given her out of her apron pocket. She opened the first doll and took out the second, then opened that and took out little tiny Kookolka, to whom Vassilisa would say:

"Eat up quickly, little one,
Then tell me, please, what should be done!"

No matter how hungry she was, Vassilisa always saved a few crumbs for her little doll, and the doll always had the answer to her troubles. If the soup needed to be cooked, Kookolka told Vassilisa to polish the pot until she could see her own face. This done, the pot cooked the soup all by itself. And if Vassilisa painted the ax to look fancy, as her doll told her to, it chopped the logs for her; while a kind word to the grain set it scattering itself across the yard for the hungry chickens.

The sun made Vassilisa's cheeks glow with health, and the snow and rain washed her skin until it was as soft and clear as a baby's. She became more beautiful with each passing day, and each day her stepsisters hated her a little more. Of course that made them even uglier than before, but what can you do with such people?

One day the blacksmith told them he had to go away to find new work, for there was no money left. He had heard of a rich tsarevich who lived beyond the thrice-nine realms and who needed a blacksmith. He told his family they would have to live in a

smaller cottage by the forest until his return. As he said goodbye to his wife he warned her not to let the children into the forest, for this was the place where Baba-Yaga Bony-Legs the witch lived, and she could eat children up in the wink of an eye.

Well, no sooner had they arrived at the cottage than Vassilisa's stepmother sent her into the forest to find berries for their supper. All night Vassilisa filled her apron with berries, but then found she had lost her way. So Vassilisa opened up her dolls, and when she had taken out Kookolka, she gave her some berries and said:

"Eat up quickly, little one,
Then tell me, please, what should be done!"

The doll told her to ask the first person she saw for the path home. Whether it was a long time or not I can't be sure, but soon enough a horseman came galloping toward her. His horse was white, and he was dressed all in silver and was so bright it hurt to look at him.

"Please, Horseman," said Vassilisa, "show me the way home."

The horseman did not speak but set his longbow and fired an arrow across the sky. Where it had passed, the trees parted to make a path. Vassilisa could just make out the cottage at the end of it and so ran quickly back home.

"Tell me, Kookolka, who was that?" asked Vassilisa.

"It was the silver horseman, bringer of Bright Morning."

The two stepsisters and their mother could not believe their eyes when they saw Vassilisa returned from the forest so soon. Right away, Vassilisa was sent deeper into the forest, to fetch mushrooms for breakfast. Vassilisa soon filled her apron with mushrooms, but it was so dark in the forest she became lost. She took out Kookolka, gave her a mushroom, and said:

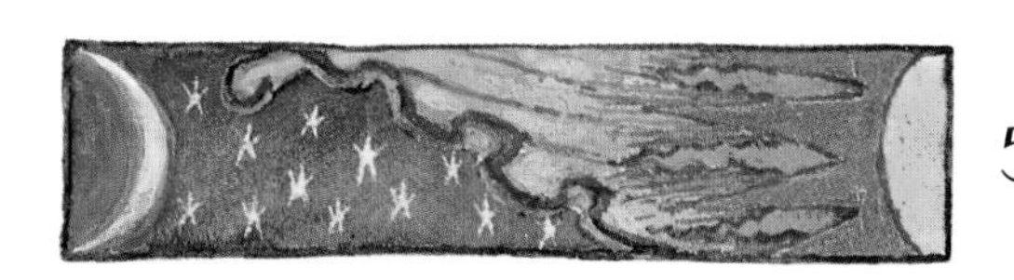

"Eat up quickly, little one,
Then tell me, please, what should be done!"

Again, the little doll told her to ask the first person she saw for the path home. Whether it was a long time or not, who knows? But soon enough Vassilisa saw another horseman galloping through the forest. He was riding a red horse, and all his armor was of gleaming gold, and he shone more brightly even than the first horseman. Vassilisa bowed her head and said:

"Please, Horseman, which path will take me home?"

He said nothing but set his longbow and fired a flaming arrow. Where it passed, the trees drew back, making a pathway to the cottage. Vassilisa ran off at once, before she lost sight of her way.

"Tell me, little doll," she said, "who was that?"

"It was the golden horseman, bringer of Glowing Daytime."

It was suppertime when Vassilisa walked through the door, and the stepmother and her two daughters nearly choked upon their food when they saw her again. They took the mushrooms, but barely gave Vassilisa a scrap to eat. Nevertheless Vassilisa put the little she was given in her apron pocket.

Seeing they needed to be more cunning, the stepmother and sisters devised a plan. As soon as it grew dark, the stepmother lit the candles and then set all three daughters a task. Her own two daughters were told to sew and knit, but Vassilisa was told to weave upon a little wooden loom. After an hour had passed, the mother let a draft from the window extinguish the candles.

"How dark it is! I cannot see," she said. "One of you must ask a neighbor for a light."

"I can see quite well enough, thank you, for my needle is bright," said the sister who sewed. "So I'm not going."

"I can see perfectly, for my needles are gleaming and sharp," said the sister who knitted. "Don't think I'm going for you."

But the wooden loom cast no light at all, so Vassilisa put a shawl around her shoulders and stepped out into the dark night.

She walked through the forest, and the trees tried to tear at her and trip her up. Soon she was lost. She took out the dolls, fed Kookolka, and said:

"Eat up quickly, little one,
Then tell me, please, what should be done!"

"You must ask the first person you see for the path to your neighbor," said Kookolka.

When it grew so dark she could no longer see the dolls in her hands, Vassilisa heard a third horseman gallop by. His horse was as black as the night, and he wore all black himself, but his cloak glittered with diamonds and his shield was silver, like the moon.

"Please, Horseman, tell me the way to my neighbor's house," whispered the Fair Vassilisa. The horseman said nothing but set his bow and fired an arrow through the black sky. The trees parted and the horseman vanished.

"Who was that?" said Vassilisa to her doll.

"It was the black horseman, bringer of Midnight."

Vassilisa saw a hut on chicken's legs at the end of the path. The fence around it was made from bones, and on each post was a skull, the eyes of which glowed with a strange, terrible light. Vassilisa dared not go on, but found the trees had closed together behind her so that she could not turn back.

An old hag stuck her head out of a window. Her nose was so hooked it almost touched her chin, and her iron teeth sent sparks out of her mouth as she gnashed them together and said:

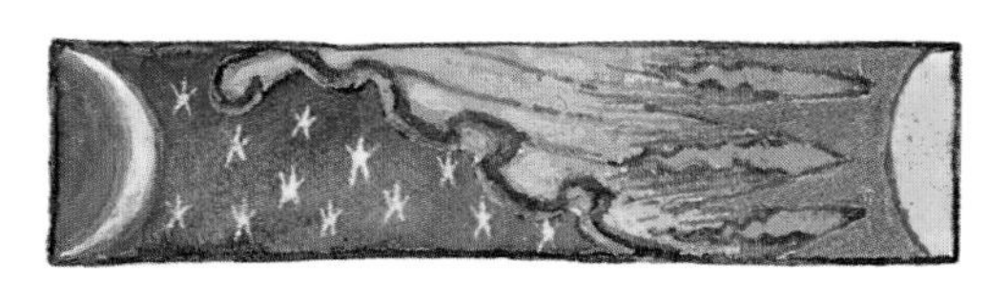

"No more water, no more mud!
Tonight I'll drink some human blood!"

Vassilisa curtsied, for she guessed this was Baba-Yaga Bony-Legs, the witch. She said in a very small voice, "Excuse me, Granny, but my stepmother has sent me for a light."

At once the bolts of teeth slid apart, and the bony gates swung open. Vassilisa walked through and up the steps to the door.

A great black crow flew down and tried to peck at the poor girl. "Leave her, Voronooshka!" said Baba-Yaga. "She enters with me!"

Inside the hut sat a bear with many teeth, and he growled as Vassilisa walked by. "Leave the child, Misha-Masher, she enters with me!"

In one corner sat a black cat. It spat at Vassilisa, but Baba-Yaga spat back. "Leave her, Grumble-Guts, she enters with me!" The witch put Vassilisa in front of a loom and told her to weave. "You must work for me, then we'll see about the light you have come for," she said. "Fail in your tasks and I will eat you."

"Yes, Granny," said Vassilisa, not daring to argue.

"Weave a hundred yards of silver cloth by the morning," said Baba-Yaga. "And do not think you can escape, for Grumble-Guts will scratch you, Misha-Masher will claw you, Voronooshka will peck you, and the gate will not let you pass. There is food in the pantry, if you are hungry."

Then Baba-Yaga left Fair Vassilisa in the hut and flew

off upon a great pestle and mortar, sweeping away her trail of pestle grindings with a broom.

Vassilisa wept into her hands, for although she was a fine weaver, she knew she could not manage such a task on her own. Quickly, she took out her dolls and said to Kookolka:

"Eat up quickly, little one,
Then tell me, please, what should be done!"

But when she opened the pantry, all she found was a little dust. She burst once more into tears, for what could her doll eat?

"Dry your eyes, Fair Vassilisa, I can eat rice," said Kookolka, and when Vassilisa looked again she saw it was rice, not dust, that lay upon the pantry shelf. "Leave some food at the window for bright morning," said the doll, "and all will be well."

This Vassilisa did, and trusting her doll, she slept for a while. As she slept the horseman of silver passed by, and when she awoke she found a hundred yards of silver cloth upon the windowsill.

Baba-Yaga returned with the dawn, and she was gnashing her iron teeth ready to eat Vassilisa. You cannot guess how angry she was to see the silver cloth, all one hundred yards of it! Furious, she set another task.

"Weave a hundred yards of golden cloth by the end of the day," snarled the witch. "If you fail I will eat you. There is food in the pantry if you are hungry."

Vassilisa watched her fly off upon the pestle and mortar, sweeping with her broom behind her. Poor Vassilisa knew she could not escape, for Voronooshka, Misha-Masher, and Grumble-Guts all watched her with staring eyes, and she could never get past the gate. Vassilisa took out Kookolka and said:

"Eat up quickly, little one,
Then tell me, please, what should be done!"

But when she opened the pantry all she could see was a stone. She wept, for she could not feed her doll with a stone.

"Dry your eyes, Fair Vassilisa, for I can eat cake all right!" said Kookolka. Vassilisa looked again and saw that it was indeed cake in the pantry. They ate it together while Kookolka told her what to do: "Leave some food at the window, for the daytime." This Vassilisa did before lying upon the hearth to sleep a while.

As she slept, the golden horseman rode by. Vassilisa awoke just as the day faded, and there upon the sill lay a hundred yards of golden cloth.

So Baba-Yaga returned to find her meal was still not ready! Right away she set yet another task. "Weave a hundred yards of black silk cloth embroidered with diamonds before midnight, or I will eat you," she said. "And there is food in the pantry if you are hungry." Then she flew off once more.

Vassilisa took out Kookolka and said:

"Eat up quickly, little one,
Then tell me, please, what should be done!"

But there were only dry leaves and sticks of wood in the pantry, and Vassilisa burst into tears.

"Dry your eyes," said the doll. "I am looking forward to our feast." When Vassilisa looked again she saw cakes, bread, pies, meat and fish, and all sorts of treats and fine foods. Eating a pancake with Kookolka, she listened to the doll's advice.

"Leave food at the window for midnight," she said. "Then all will be well."

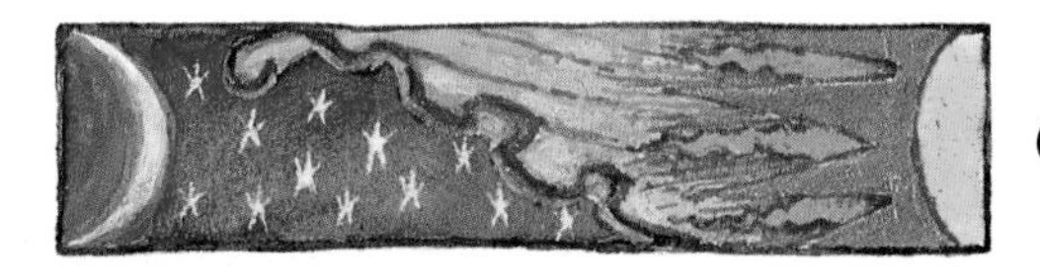

This done, Vassilisa slept as the black horseman passed by. When she awoke, Vassilisa saw a hundred yards of black silk cloth embroidered with diamonds upon the windowsill.

On her return Baba-Yaga spun around and screamed in fury. She told Vassilisa she would eat her in any case, in the morning, because she did not like clever girls, especially not pretty ones.

As soon as the witch was asleep, Vassilisa gave Kookolka a few pieces of the food from the pantry and said through her tears:

"Eat up quickly, little one,
Then tell me please, what should be done!"

"Dry your eyes," said the doll "and let us feast with our old friends, Voronooshka, Misha-Masher, and Grumble-Guts."

So Vassilisa gathered up the silk cloths and walked toward Grumble-Guts, who spat and growled at her. She threw the poor animal a fish, and so astonished was the cat that she lay down at Vassilisa's feet and purred, letting her walk past. Then Vassilisa found a pie, and she gave this to the bear. He rolled onto his back and let her through the door. Then Vassilisa gave a cake to the crow, and he flew up to his nest and let her pass.

Quickly, Vassilisa ran to the bony gates, but they would not let her through. She wept, for she could not feed a gate and she knew that bright morning would soon awaken Baba-Yaga. Her tears fell upon the hinges and all at once the gates swung open. Vassilisa ran quickly through, but it was so dark in the forest! Bravely she took a glowing skull from Baba-Yaga's fence, and when she held it up the trees parted to make a path.

You have no idea how angry Baba-Yaga was when she awoke and saw that her breakfast had escaped.

"Why did my gates let her pass?" she growled.

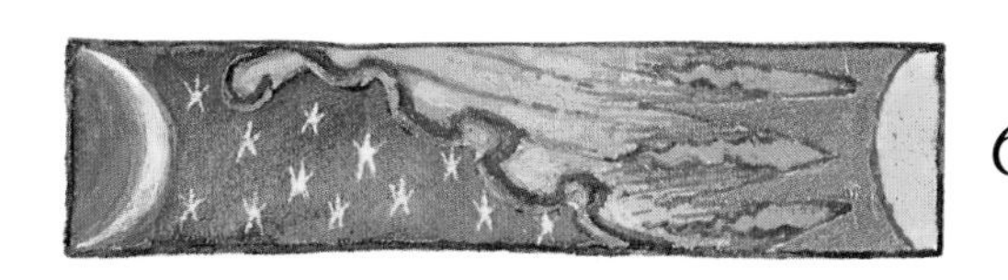

"We could not keep her, for she wept over us," said the gates.

"Why, Voronooshka, did you not peck her to death?" snarled Baba-Yaga.

"Why? Because she fed me with cake, and you are too stingy to spare even a worm!" And the crow spread its wings and flew away.

"Misha-Masher!" screeched the old witch. "Why did you not claw the girl to death?"

"She gave me a whole pie," said the bear. "You never gave me so much as a stale crust!" And he leaped from the doorway and ran off into the forest.

"Grumble-Guts!" howled Baba-Yaga. "Why did you not scratch her to death?"

"Because she was kind to me and gave me a whole fish," said the cat. "Yet after years of hard work you've never given me even a single bone!" And the cat ran for the door. But Baba-Yaga was too quick and caught poor Grumble-Guts. She tied the cat up with a golden chain, put her into a casket of oak, and hurled it into the sea.

It was night when Vassilisa reached her father's cottage, and as she opened the door her stepmother and sisters ran to welcome her. "We are so glad to see you," said the stepsisters, trembling. "Ever since you left, every flame, every candle has died before our eyes!"

"It has been like midnight for every hour since you went," said the stepmother, and it seemed that only the fire of Baba-Yaga Bony-Legs could burn there. But the eyes of the glowing skull stared hard at them and scared them. They did not know how to control the fire of a witch.

"It burns me!" they wailed, and fierce tongues of flame darted out, snatching at their clothes. They hid behind chairs and threw water at the skull. But they could not escape the magic fire of Baba-Yaga, which swallowed them up.

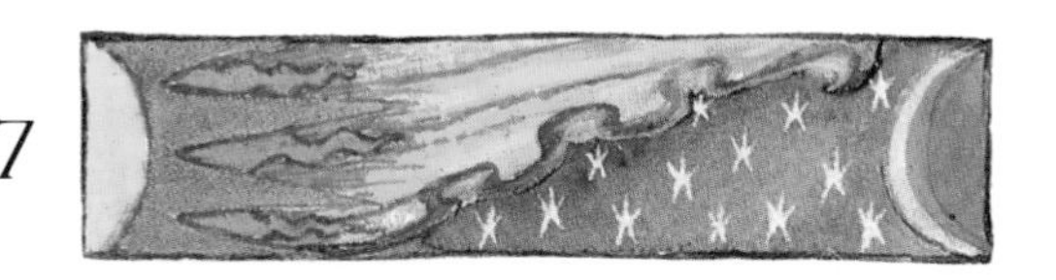

Vassilisa was quite untouched by all this, and her silk cloths and her dolls were unharmed. She buried the skull in the garden, and when she looked up she saw her father, home that day of all days! He wept not a single tear for his cruel wife and unkind stepdaughters when Vassilisa told him the true tale.

They went off beyond the thrice-nine lands to the tsardom of the tsarevich who had made Vassilisa's father his blacksmith. Vassilisa stayed home and wove fine silks, and her father worked at the smithy by the palace stables.

One day the tsarevich announced that he needed some new shirts. The blacksmith told him his own daughter could weave finer cloth than any that might be bought. The tsarevich agreed to sample her work, and so the blacksmith rushed home and told Fair Vassilisa to start weaving. But instead, Vassilisa took out the cloth of the midnight horseman and made fine shirts for the tsarevich. He was so pleased with the result that he

demanded that his coronation cloak be made by Vassilisa.

So that very day Vassilisa took out the golden cloth and made the tsarevich a coronation cloak. He was delighted, and after being crowned as the tsar, he ordered the smith's daughter to make a wedding dress, for a tsar must have a wife. Vassilisa worked all through the night and by the next day had made a magnificent dress of silver, with a veil like bright dawn.

The tsar was overjoyed and demanded to see the smith's daughter. So Vassilisa, in her apron and simple dress, stood before the tsar. He was struck by her beauty and asked her to try on the wedding dress she had made. It fitted perfectly, and they were married that very day.

The tsar never guessed how his pretty wife had made such fine clothes. Vassilisa said nothing, but she always left food on the windowsill, each morning, during the day, and at midnight. Of course, the tsar and Fair Vassilisa lived a long and happy life together and never once needed Kookolka's help. Even so, Vassilisa kept her mother's gift in her pocket, always remembering to leave a little food there, just in case.

V

Tsar Saltan and Koshka the Cat

KOSHKA WASHED behind her ears and stretched her back in a long, graceful arch. No one said anything at all, so Koshka narrowed her huge green eyes and said, "Now then, did you like the tale or not?"

"Oh yes! The bit about the food," said the merchants.

"The bit about the beautiful Vassilisa," said Guidon.

"The bit about the wicked stepsisters," said Militrissa.

"Good, I can go to sleep now," said Koshka, and she curled up into a black ball of fur. Then she opened an eye. "I shall expect that fish when I wake up," she said, yawning. "The biggest and tastiest fish was the promise!"

"I'll go right away," said Guidon, picking up his spear. He bade farewell to the old merchant and ran down to the beach.

"We must leave," said the merchant to Militrissa. "Now I have at last heard the tale of Baba-Yaga, I long to relate it to Tsar Saltan."

"Then give my greeting to the tsar," said Militrissa, "and remind him that you heard the tale from Koshka."

"We shall tell him, my lady, and I am certain he will accept your invitation this time, for the cat is a wonder without equal!"

Guidon watched the merchants set sail as he waited to catch Koshka a nice big fish. None swam by, so he wandered a bit

farther along the beach. Still he could see no fish.

Instead, though, he saw seven white swans flying across the blue sky, and at their tails flew a monstrous eagle. Guidon quickly threw his lance at the pursuer, and with a cry it fell into the sea and vanished. The swans circled the island and landed upon the sea. Guidon was much taken with them, for they were very graceful and as white as snow.

One of them wore a golden crown. It swam over to Guidon and said, "You saved us from our tormentor, and we are truly grateful. How can we repay your kindness?"

"Beautiful swan, I know not what to ask!" said Guidon, unsure how a swan — even one with a crown — could help him.

"Ask what you desire and then see," said the swan. "I can help you only three times, so think wisely."

"Well, the sea is empty of fish, and my desire at the moment is to catch one for my friend, Koshka the cat," said Guidon.

The swan flapped her wings, and there at Guidon's feet lay a large silver fish, already baked. Guidon thanked the swan and rushed across the island to give Koshka her fish before it got cold. Militrissa ate too, and Koshka said it was indeed the biggest and tastiest of fish. But Guidon did not stay to eat. The swan awaited his second wish, and he knew already what it should be.

"Swan-White, my greatest desire is to see my father," he said. "But there is never room on the merchant's ship for a prince."

"A prince too big to cross the sea
Is better off a bumblebee,"

said the swan, and she flapped her wings.

Where Guidon had stood, a bee buzzed. It was a little unsure of itself, as it was not used to being a bee and having so many legs. Yet

a bee it was, and it buzzed and hummed across the sparkling blue sea and quickly caught up with the merchant's ship. It disappeared through a tiny gap between the planks on the deck, and no one was any the wiser.

The ship sailed across the seven seas and beyond the thrice-nine lands to the tsardom of Tsar Saltan the Magnificent. The merchants came ashore and presented the foods they had brought to the tsar. As usual there was a great banquet, to which Katooshka and Liza Poffarikha came, giggling and excited. Surely now the tsar would cast the merchant into the sea. And they were so excited that they did not notice a little black and yellow bee as it flew through an open window and hid behind a curtain.

"Did you hear the story?" the tsar asked the merchants. "Did you find out the tale of Baba-Yaga the witch?"

"We sailed beyond the thrice-nine realms and over the seven seas," said the old merchant. "We asked in every port but no one knew the tale. At last we returned to the Isle of Bouyan, where the fair lady and her golden-haired son sat beneath the oak tree with their friend the wise cat. We asked the cat to tell us this tale."

"But I dare say she did not know it," sighed the tsar.

"Oh yes, mighty Tsar, she knew the tale and, believe me, it was worth the long search."

The tsar was overjoyed. "Well, my friends, tell me the tale of Baba-Yaga and Vassilisa, for I have waited long enough to hear it."

"Of course, great Tsar," said the old merchant, and he sat down and told the whole of the tale, adding, "Truly this cat is without compare, for no storyteller I have ever heard could equal her."

"Then I must accept this invitation and hear her for myself!" said the tsar. He ordered his bags to be packed and declared that he would set sail that very night.

The two sisters gaped and gasped, and neither could believe her ears. Baba-Yaga's own story! How could this cat know all that the witch knew? Quicker than quick, they hitched up their skirts and ran on their spindly legs through the forest to Baba-Yaga.

"Here's something strange," thought Guidon as he watched his two aunts flee. He darted out of the window and followed them, through the twisted thorny trees. They all arrived outside the hut on chicken's legs at about the same time. From inside came a noise like a rusty saw cutting metal. It was the old hag, Baba-Yaga Bony-Legs, snoring fit to burst.

Katooshka and Liza Poffarikha rattled her bony gates to wake her, and she leaped up off the stone slab where she slept and stuck her ugly face out of the window.

"You again!" she growled. "How much longer am I supposed to hide these tsarevich-princes for you? They'll soon fill the whole hut. Why, I should gobble you both up!"

The two sisters began to babble, but the witch was too angry to listen to it.

"Come in and tell me what's what," she snarled.

But the sisters got no farther, for Guidon was no fool. Guessing what had become of his six brothers, he buzzed around his aunts, and when they opened their mouths to scream, he stung each upon the tongue. Having done this, he sped after Baba-Yaga. She shut her window, so Guidon-bee flew through a crack in the door. Baba-Yaga swung her broom at him and cursed and spat. But Guidon-bee stung her in the eye, and he was so small she could no longer see him.

She saw the two sisters, though, wailing and moaning about their swollen tongues, so she leaped out of her door and took to them instead.

"This is your fault!" she screamed, thrashing them mercilessly. "Come back here so that I can smash you to pieces!"

Meanwhile, Guidon found a hidden cage made all of human bones. In it sat the six tsarevich-princes, each one a brother to the tsarevich-bee. He said, as loudly as a bee can:

"Put my feet upon the floor,
Let me be a prince once more!"

At once he was Tsarevich Guidon again, and his six brothers saw in him the look they saw in each other's eyes, so they knew he was their own dear brother come to save them. Six had been unable to break the cage, but now that they were seven they smashed the bones and scrambled out. Guidon embraced them all, then they climbed upon Baba-Yaga's pestle and mortar and took to the skies.

But they could not take Baba-Yaga's broom to wipe away the trail of pestle grindings, for she was still using it to thrash their aunts. As soon as the princes were in the air, the old witch heard the pestle and mortar fly past.

"Ho!" she screamed, letting go of the sisters. "Who steals from me? I shall eat them whole!" And she leaped upon her broom, which sped through the air after the princes. They pummeled ever harder with the pestle and mortar, grinding and pounding their way across the sky, for seven princes can go faster than one witch. The old hag howled and screamed with rage, for with only one good eye she could not steer between the gnarled, twisted trees. She struck a branch and was sent spinning into the air. Down she came, the horrid old crone, down through the sky and into an almost bottomless ravine, which was so deep and so wide it took her a hundred and one years to climb out.

Katooshka and Liza Poffarikha ran all the way back to the

palace, only to find the tsar boarding his ship. One clung to his legs, the other held his arms. But as neither could say a word with their swollen tongues, they could not stop the tsar from sailing, and off he went.

All this time the princes pummeled. Across the thrice-nine lands they sped, and then across the seven seas and beyond, until they reached the Island of Bouyan where Militrissa and Koshka waited.

Militrissa had never imagined such joy as she felt when she set eyes on Guidon, for whom she had searched without pause since he had disappeared from the island. And her joy was sevenfold, for there with him were his six princely brothers. And Militrissa wept a thousand tears for each day they had been parted from her. Yet the princes barely had time to relate their story and enjoy their mother's warm embrace before Militrissa caught sight of a bright ship, sailing upon the blue sea.

It was the ship of Tsar Saltan Saltanovich from beyond the thrice-nine realms, together with the merchants, who led him to the Island of Bouyan. Militrissa did not know what to do, for was this not the same man who had cast her into the sea? She and her seven heroic sons hid behind the broad trunk of the mighty oak until they could see what sort of mood the tsar was in.

Tsar Saltan Saltanovich climbed the hill and found Koshka sitting in the tree. He tickled her behind her ear and said, "Tell me a tale, clever cat, if you can."

"I know just the tale for you," said the wise cat. "A tale about a tsar who cast his wife into the sea."

"Go on," said the tsar, who felt a sharp pain in his heart.

"It's the tale about the tsaritsa whose sisters stole six of her seven children and gave them to a witch."

"Go on," said the tsar, barely daring to breathe.

"This is the tale of the mother who hid one son up her sleeve and was cast upon the sea with him."

"Go on!" said the tsar, clasping his breast.

"Well, the casket did not sink, and the tsaritsa and her son did not perish," said Koshka.

"But the tsaritsa bore puppies and kittens and pieces of bread, not tsarevich-princes," said Tsar Saltan, his eyes burning.

"It is no kitten that stands before you, Father," said Guidon, walking around the mighty oak. "And my brothers were taken from the cradle by my aunts and replaced by puppies, kittens, and bread."

"Then what became of your six brothers?" asked the tsar, tears running down his face.

"They stand before you, Father!" said the six brothers, revealing themselves. "Neither puppies nor kittens nor pieces of bread, we have been the sons of a witch all this time."

"Then what became of your mother, who was so cruelly wronged by her foolish tsar?" said Saltan, weeping.

"She stands before you, husband dear!" said Militrissa, and she walked around the tree and bowed down before the tsar.

"Do not bow before me," said Saltan. "It is I who kneel before you!" And the tsar knelt down and kissed Militrissa's hand. "Can you forgive my foolishness?"

And she could, for she knew it was neither a fault of hers nor of his, but of her sisters, whom she had loved and trusted. The tsar then greeted each son and wept a thousand tears for each day they had been parted from him. And after he had embraced his father, Guidon went to ask his last gift of the swan, for he now knew what his greatest desire was.

"Swan-White, I have heard tales of maidens patient and faithful,

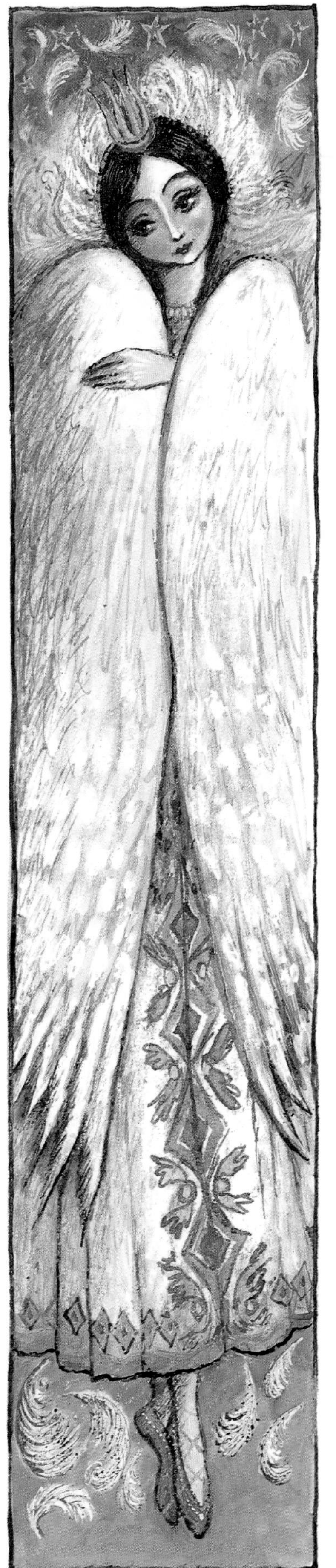

and I have heard about a princess whose loveliness was inexhaustible, and about a maiden as fair as she was kind. Can such a maiden exist, and if so, where can I find her?"

"Can you love this maiden without seeing her?" asked the swan.

"If she is as kind as you, I can love her truly!" said Guidon.

Hearing this, the swan flapped her wings and vanished, and in her place stood a princess, with a golden crown, whose beauty put the sun to shame and who outshone the fullest moon. And the six swans vanished too, becoming maidens of almost equal loveliness.

"Where is Swan-White?" cried Guidon.

"She stands before you," said the princess. "Your vow has freed me from being a swan forever. When you struck down the eagle, you destroyed a demon. I would not love this evil spirit, and so he cursed myself and my sisters and caused us to remain as swans until I had a pledge of true love. I was given just three chances — your three wishes — to find this promise."

Guidon took the Princess Swan-White by the hand. "Then I am glad it was I who had the wishes, for you are truly my heart's desire."

Upon the hill, around the mighty oak tree, there was a scene of great joy and happiness. The whole tale was told, and all the tears that had been shed were dried and forgotten.

"There is one thing I have yet to understand," said the tsar. "How is it the cat knows the stories of the witch so well?"

"Kind Koshka," said Guidon to the puss. "Where did you learn such enchantments?"

"Tsarevich, you know the answer already, for did I not tell you Baba-Yaga's tale?"

"Of course," said the prince, "and beautifully too."

"Then you remember what became of Voronooshka the crow?"

"He ate the cake and flew away," said Guidon.

"And Misha-Masher the bear?"

"Ate the pie and ran into the forest."

"And Grumble-Guts?"

"Was wrapped in chains, put in an oak casket, and cast into the sea," said Guidon.

"Ah! but the casket did not sink, and it sailed the seven seas until it came apart on a beach. The casket grew green shoots and became a mighty oak tree, and the chain of gold ran through the branches, and on the end of it..."

"Grumble-Guts!" said everyone together.

"I learned quickly and I learned well from the old witch, and she told me her most powerful magic: her stories!" said the clever cat. "Now you understand why the one about old Baba-Yaga Bony-Legs was unpleasant to recall."

"And how did you know what became of Vassilisa?" asked Guidon.

"Dawn, Daytime, and Midnight pass by us all if we only take the time to notice," said Koshka. "They told me what became of their friend Vassilisa."

"Well then, Koshka, let us free you from this prison, for you have earned that at least," said the tsar.

So the tsar and the seven tsarevich-princes pulled and pulled at the golden chain, and all agreed it was the strongest chain they had ever come across. But at last the gold broke, the chains fell out of

the branches, and Koshka was free. She purred loudly and licked them all, for never was there a happier cat in all of Russia.

And then, without further delay, they all said goodbye to the Island of Bouyan and set sail.

Over the seven seas and beyond the thrice-nine realms they sailed, to the tsardom of Saltan Saltanovich. And who was waiting there? Katooshka and Liza Poffarikha. They knelt before their little sister, weeping, wailing, and blaming their lies on Baba-Yaga the witch, their tongues being somewhat improved. But the tsar was deaf to their pleas and would not allow even his beloved and beautiful wife to change his mind.

The two sisters were bundled into a casket and hurled from the highest cliff into the deepest ocean. But the Tsar of the Sea was not as tolerant as he sometimes is, and so the casket sank without a trace and neither sister was ever seen again.

You can imagine the scenes in the palace the next day, for not only did Guidon marry the enchanted Princess Swan-White, but her six swan-maidens had fallen in love with his brothers on the voyage, and they too were married on that happiest of days. The bells rang, the people sang, and not a single gray cloud crossed that sunny sky!

All the folk were more, not less,
Filled with health and happiness,
They lifted up their heads to cheer,
The feast it lasted one full year.
Koshka drank and you can bet,
She fairly got her whiskers wet!
And then she told a tale or two,
As good as those she's just told you.

Author's Note

THESE TALES FROM the land of Rus (the old name for Russia) were made up long, long ago when few people could read or write. With Russia's vast lakes, deep forests, and long, cold winters, it's easy to see how stories about snowmaidens, water sprites, wolves, and witches were invented. The stories people told often involved godlike characters, such as the spirits of Winter and Spring in *The Snowmaiden*. Then with the introduction of Christianity into Russia came new figures, like St. Nikolai in *Sadko the Minstrel*.

Each time a tale was told, it would be a little bit different, depending on who was telling it—whether a royal storyteller at the palace, or a wise *babooshka* (Russian for "grandmother") at her grandchild's bedside. The first person to collect and write down the stories was Alexander Afanasiev, whose books inspired other Russian writers, artists, and composers. *The Firebird* became a famous ballet by Stravinsky, and Rimsky-Korsakov wrote fairy-tale operas based on *Tsar Saltan*, *The Snowmaiden,* and *Sadko*—showing that there are many different ways of retelling a story.

But I expect you are wondering why the stories in this book are told by a cat. There are several Russian tales about a magical storytelling cat. The most famous is in a poem by Alexander Pushkin called "Ruslan and Ludmilla." Of course, Koshka (her name means "cat" in Russian) knows hundreds of stories, but I've chosen the four I think are the best and retold them, adding a few new touches—just like the storytellers of old.

Most of the names in the book are traditional, but I made up a few of my own, derived from Russian words:

Katooshka is thin and sews—her name means "spindle."
Kookolka means "little doll."
Liza Poffarikha means "sly fox, the cook."
Misha-Masher is from Misha, a Russian nickname for a bear.
Voronooshka means "little crow."